The Lost 1

# of Malplaquet

Andrew Dalton

illustrated by
Jonny Boatfield

*Carey:
Thank you so much for all your work and kindness.
Andrew*

The Lutterworth Press

For Lilliputians everywhere

First Published in 2007 by
The Lutterworth Press
P.O. Box 60
Cambridge
CB1 2NT

www.Lutterworth.com
Publishing@Lutterworth.com

ISBN: 978 0 7188 3049 6 hardback
ISBN: 978 0 7188 3050 2 paperback

British Library Cataloguing in Publication Data:
A Catalogue Record is available from the British Library

The Malplaquet Trilogy takes much of its initial inspiration
from *Mistress Masham's Repose*, one of the less known work
of the great English writer, T.H. White

Printed in England by
Athenaeum Press, Gateshead

Contents

The Prophecy

A Child no more, the Man appears,
He comes of Age, the Hope of Years.
Our Fount of Wisdom, whose Way is Delight,
True Source of all Pure Knowledge and Insight,
Our Guide, for whom the Bells do Ring,
Thy Presence much Warmth in Friendship Bring.
Thou makest the Sea-people great Appear,
This Blessed Island shalt have no Fear.
In every Quarter defend our Shores,
Unite our People, grow strong in Wars.
The Capital gained, our Frontiers Sealed,
Temples Restored, the Nation Healed.
Through thee the Great Empire newly Starts,
The Garden Kingdom, true Home of our Hearts.

after Alexander Pope

Chapter 1: First Moves

Hurrying head-down through 'China and Glassware' in the smartest Department store in Oxford, Julius Newbold felt confused, lonely and nervous.

He felt confused because two weeks ago, whilst happily boating on the lake at Malplaquet, he had been attacked by a group of tiny humans only six inches high, savaged by an extremely vicious local fish (a dreaded Vazedir), chained to one of the old garden buildings, and ridiculed by the visitors as a half-crazed hermit who'd been hired to entertain them. Finally, he had been roughly ejected from the gardens by an irritating little man with a little badge.

And before all these humiliations, he'd been hiding for months in a smelly and leaky tent in Malplaquet's miserable woods, and the smell still wouldn't go away.

And that of course explained why he was lonely. Everywhere he went, people backed off when they realised the source of the awful stench.

He quickly glanced around the store; it was happening yet again. Shoppers were casually walking towards him, then suddenly halting a few yards away, screwing their noses up and diving down the nearest side-aisle. He spotted an anxious assistant on the phone looking in his direction and obviously warning other departments of his movements. He knew that his smell *was* absolutely foul; a rancid and pungent mixture of rotting vegetation, animal droppings, dank clothes and mould. He had tried everything to rid himself of the odour; showering every day (twice), scraping himself with a scary implement from the Far East that removed two layers of skin (one dead and one live), even driving through his local Car Wash with all the windows down.

Nothing had worked. He now had the up-escalator all to himself, and people were bounding down the adjacent one. Reaching the top and stepping off, he pulled out of his pocket the bright yellow piece of paper, read the words (again), looked at his watch (again) – 10.55 – and made his way towards the café.

That piece of paper was precisely why he was nervous.

When he'd seen the colour of the note dropping through his let-ter-box yesterday morning, he had involuntarily flinched. It hadn't needed a signature; the colour was sufficient. The terseness of the message was also familiar: *Shoppers' Rest. 11 am. Tomorrow.*

For the hundredth time since that final series of incidents at Malplaquet, he turned over in his mind that fateful moment when, chained up and furiously angry and frustrated, he had so stupidly (and so loudly) shouted out that one word. That name.

Biddle.

There were bound to be extremely serious repercussions.

In the café, preoccupied by his anxious thoughts, he wandered along past the food counter, absent-mindedly placing the occasional item on his tray. At the pay-desk, the young girl looked quizzically at his unusual collection; an empty cup, two serviettes, a bottle of water, a plastic fork, a sachet of tomato sauce, and two small blocks of butter. Raising her hand over her nose and mouth, she said a muffled, '90p.' Julius dropped a one-pound coin on the desk and hurried off to a corner-seat.

At the very same moment as he sat down, three large men in dark suits approached the manager, who was standing by the café entrance. One spoke with him. Nodding in acknowledgement, he immediately clipped a rope across the passage-way and briskly gestured to his staff. Those behind the counters simply left through a side door, whilst two others quickly and quietly approached all the customers. A few words were said to each, vouchers were handed over, and within a minute of his arrival Julius had the café all to himself. Apart from the three other men.

His nervousness increased ten-fold.

The largest of the trio, with a small black listening-device curved round one ear, strode over to Julius' table and squeezed his frame into the seat opposite. Hands clenched together on the table in a wad of thick fingers, he looked straight at Julius, who was unable to return the stare. Nothing was said. Julius could feel himself beginning to sweat.

The silent tension was suddenly interrupted by the sound of the lift doors opening around the corner. The big man stiffened, and a phone rang inside his jacket. The guard reached inside, took the call and handed the phone to Julius, indicating that he should lift it to his ear.

The voice was unmistakable, cold and characteristically blunt.

'Do *not* turn round, and do *not* attempt to speak. Just enjoy your little snack, although your choices surprise me. You seem distracted.' In the slight pause, Julius was aware of a small bead of perspiration running down his neck. The calm and measured tone continued. 'A most unfortunate end to the first plan. *Most* unfortunate. But perhaps not – how shall I put it? – *unexpected*, given your past record. We must not forget, however, that you still have your sight, and therefore your uses – and you still have your debts.' Julius shifted position awkwardly. 'You will remain in service at Malplaquet, and you will receive further instructions. In the meantime, take very good care of those eyes, but I don't wish to see that face of yours ever again. That is your next task.'

The phone went dead. Julius, anxious and bewildered, slowly handed it back. He was given in return a small business card. At the top it stated, '*Altered Images Inc.*' and underneath, '*Specialists in corrective and cosmetic surgery, physical restructuring and facial reconstruction.*' Below that was an address and Freephone number. Julius shuddered.

The dark-suited gorilla leaned over. 'Word of advice, mate.' He paused and grimaced. 'Do us all a favour. Have a bath when you get home.'

Jamie Thompson was wandering through the gardens surrounding Malplaquet School (which he'd soon be joining), to visit an old family friend, whom they called 'Granny.' This summer she had introduced him to the Lilliputians living in the garden's 'temples', and had also explained that he was the long-awaited leader (the 'Guide'), who could unite their four provinces and bring about the new Empire. Jamie was holding up to his ear a mobile phone that had stopped working months ago.

'Any idea why she wants this meeting, Nigriff?'

'None at all, young master,' came the reply from inside Jamie's right sleeve. 'But I believe that the great General Thorclan will also be present.'

'That's very generous of you, Nigriff,' said Jamie. 'You wouldn't have called him 'great' a few weeks ago.'

'Not correct, sir. I've always had the most enormous respect for the General and his fine troops in the Grecian province.'

'Right,' replied Jamie. 'Which is why you once called them "savages and barbarians," I suppose?'

'If I *did* use those specific words – and I'm not convinced that is the case – you must have misunderstood the context, Master Jamie. I would have been describing their *opponents'* opinion of their awesome fighting qualities.'

Not for the first time, Jamie realised there was no point in trying to out-argue Nigriff, who always had the last word. The 'Permanent Grand Archivist' lived in the province of Elysium, which meant he was naturally clever and articulate. (The other provinces also had particular types of people; the people in Palladia were very practical, the Cascadians sporting, and the Grecians – like Thorclan – were the soldiers).

Jamie was pleased that the Lilliputians were now (at last) speaking *warmly* about other provincials – and actually visiting each other, which they hadn't done for years. And when they did, some temples were mysteriously affecting the visitors; Thorclan had said something very clever inside an Elysian one, and Nigriff had begun rowing like an expert oarsman near a lakeside temple in Cascadia.

It was all extremely odd.

Jamie and Nigriff walked through the Bell Gate on Malplaquet's perimeter and approached Granny's cottage, built onto the back of a classical pavilion by the Octagon Lake. The old lady herself was in her front yard with their teenage friend, Vicky, poking around amongst the collection of tubs and stone ornaments.

Vicky had lifted to one side the figure of a toga-clad woman carrying a water jar, and was now picking up a small statue of a seated lion. 'I can't hear anything, I'm afraid,' she said. 'You said it was a sort of humming?'

'Or perhaps a soft buzz,' replied Granny. 'As if a bee was stuck somewhere. Oh, hello, Jamie, I didn't see you.' She stood up straight, pressing her aching back and giving him a friendly scowl. 'I don't know, young people nowadays, can't go anywhere without their mobiles.'

'It's not what you think, Granny,' said Jamie, still holding his arm up to his ear. 'This one doesn't work.'

'That makes it even worse,' replied Granny. 'You could have an obsessive ailment in your arm. It might need treatment. '

'It's not been called an obsessive ailment before,' said Jamie, smirking, 'but you might be right about treatment.'

Nigriff's head poked out. 'I do apologise, did I miss something?'

Vicky grinned at him. 'I think Granny said you're an observant sailman and she wants to treat you . . . .'

'Most kind, Madam. However, despite my recent rowing exploits on the water, I am still primarily an Archivist. But I *do* like the sound of a treat.'

'Let's go in then,' smiled Granny. 'Thorclan's been here a while. I've been trying to explain a few things to him, but I'm not sure he understands yet.'

Facing away from them, the General was standing on the polished table, feet apart and his hands clasped behind him.

'At ease, General,' announced Jamie.

'Thank you, sir,' replied the old soldier, turning round, 'but I already was.' He clicked his heels smartly on the smooth surface and saluted. Granny winced at her best table being stamped on. Jamie held out his index finger, which Thorclan grasped and shook warmly.

'Let's make a start,' said Granny. 'I did ask Yenech to come, but now he's been granted the Freedom of Malplaquet, he could be anywhere.' The others smiled, remembering Yenech being decorated at the recent Provincial Assembly, in honour of his bravery in the battle with Old Smelly on the lakes. It was a most suitable award; he was well-known for wandering (by mistake) all over the gardens.

The adults each adjusted their chairs, and the two Lilliputians made themselves comfortable on squashy pincushions (minus the pins) deliberately left for them on the table.

'Vicky, can you take the Minutes?' asked Granny, pushing across a pad of paper and a pen. 'It's about time we did these things properly.'

'Okay,' agreed Vicky. 'Those present?'

'Nigriff, previously Chief Historian (2nd Papyrus Division), Most Notable Librarian (First Editions), Senior Imperial Archivist, and most recently appointed as Permanent Grand Archivist.'

'Thorclan, General,' added a second. 'Leader of the Grecian Army, previously honoured as Great Lord Of Battles, and recently appointed as Supreme Commander At Battles.' He winked at Vicky. 'Just write "General Thorclan, GLOB, SCAB," if you prefer, my dear.'

'Jamie,' came a proud third voice. 'Surname Thompson, known as the Guide, and also (in no particular order) the Hope of Years, Fount of Wisdom, True Source of all Pure Knowledge and...'

'...and that's enough,' interjected Granny, glaring at the three men, who looked suitably apologetic. 'Just put our first names, Vicky, we've some serious business to sort out. Agenda Item 1,' she continued. 'Biddle. What do we know about him at the moment?'

'Same name as the eighteenth century sea-captain who rescued Gulliver and then returned to kidnap some Lilliputians,' offered Vicky. 'This one's probably a descendant. He's just tried, using Old Smelly, to capture two, one of each sex. Probably to breed them.'

'His son is starting at the school with me,' added Jamie. 'Oh yes, nearly forgot, Biddle told them he's relocating his business here.'

'Hmm,' murmured Granny, 'just what I was afraid of. He knows he can't trust any more incompetents, and he's going to do more himself. We'll have to keep our eyes and ears open.'

'And our brains,' said Thorclan, who after his a flash of inspiration in the Elysian temple, had sent some special troops to benefit from training-exercises there. On return, these soldiers had formed an Intelligence section in the Grecian Army. It hadn't had any Intelligence before.

'Absolutely,' agreed Granny, 'which brings us neatly to Agenda Item 2: The Lilliputians becoming visible, *and* changing. Who wants to lead on this one?'

'I will,' said Jamie, taking a deep breath. 'Okay, basic facts. They've been virtually invisible here for centuries, partly because they were hiding on an island, but also because Malplaquet was in such a bad state that most humans didn't sense what the place was really about. But the National Trust is now *restoring* the temples, and so the visitors are starting to feel and see things – like the craftsmanship, the atmosphere . . .'

'And tiny humans,' added Thorclan. 'Brilliant. Makes complete sense.'

'No, it doesn't,' said Jamie. 'I've got a couple of questions.'

'Exactly!' agreed Thorclan breezily. 'Not *totally* complete sense, just *almost* complete sense.'

'Question one,' continued Jamie. '*Why* did the Lilliputians become invisible? When Biddle kidnapped them nearly three hundred years ago, everybody could see them. And then it's like they faded away. Why?'

'Why indeed?' repeated Thorclan, looking round at the assembled faces, which all remained unalterably blank.

'First question – unanswered,' said Jamie. 'Try the second. Restoring the temples makes the Lilliputians visible, and also changes their character – like Thorclan becoming brainy . . . sorry, *more* brainy, in the Temple of Ancient Virtue. But the *whole garden* is being restored. So, why are the *temples* so important?'

The other faces turned towards Thorclan, who shrugged his shoulders.

'Because they're in Pope's prophecy?' suggested Vicky hopefully. (This was an old poem by the eighteenth-century writer Alexander Pope, discovered in the archives by Nigriff, which indicated that Jamie was the Guide who would bring about a mighty Empire. 'Temples restored' was a phrase in it.)

'Probably,' said Granny. 'And talking of the prophecy, there's that bit in it about 'capital gained'. We don't *really* know what that means yet.'

'Well, it means I'm starting school here,' said Jamie. 'The 'capital' *has* to be the school mansion, as it's the biggest building. There's also my idea of Malplaquet and Lilliput being similar shapes; the mansion is right where Lilliput's capital, Mildendo, was.'

As before, the others seemed unconvinced by Jamie's idea;

only Nigriff looked thoughtful. 'Your theory *does* warrant further investigation,' he said. 'If you would do me the honour, young sir, I will acquaint you with the untold riches of the Imperial Archives. They contain an ancient map of Lilliput that may be of considerable help to us.'

'Which is a good place to call this meeting to a close,' said Granny. 'Points made, questions raised, and plans laid. Any other business?'

'I do have two matters,' said Nigriff. 'The first concerns the Pebble Alcove, which, as we all know, has on occasion portrayed mysterious images of the Gulliver story. In accordance with the request of the Listener, I intend to fully investigate that building.' His words were met with nods of approval. 'The second concerns the enlightenment of my countrymen, who remain sadly unaware of their true history and heritage. As we have previously agreed, it is our privilege and responsibility to reveal that they are noble Lilliputians, people of dignity; not just tiny creatures who, by some cruel trick of nature exist in a hostile world of over-mighty giants.'

Thorclan clapped, and shouted, 'Hear, hear!'

'Which is why,' continued Nigriff, 'I will be making two presentations. Firstly, I have been given an opportunity to address the renowned Academic Board, the guardians of our intellectual life.' (Murmurs of approval.) 'Secondly, I can formally announce that my application to the Listener for a Full Speech Licence at the next Assembly has been granted. Your support at that gathering would be greatly appreciated, though it may not be straightforward.'

'Presumably you're not going to read out Pope's poetry again?' inquired Jamie, remembering how Nigriff tried to win over an unsympathetic audience by publicly declaiming the poem . . . .

'Sir, as it happens, I was considering – bearing in mind that some of his allusions are rather obscure and technical . . . .' He stopped, as he noticed four heads shaking. Thorclan took him by the arm and spoke to him gently. 'Take it from me, old chap,' he said, 'it wouldn't be very intelligent. I've done a few night-exercises in Elysium recently. I know about these things.'

Mrs Thompson, quite out of breath, came rushing in through the back door of their house, dumped her two bags of shopping and dashed into the sitting-room, startling her husband who was stretched out half-dozing on the sofa.

'You'll never guess what's happening!' she blurted out.

'In that case you'd better tell me,' answered Mr Thompson wearily, slowly sitting up and rubbing his eyes. Relaxing was such hard work sometimes.

'It's the Manor! The Harrison-Smythe's. They're moving – leaving!'

Mr Thompson took a deep breath and looked sympathetically at her. Obviously she had got the wrong end of the stick; there was no way that the Harrison-Smythes would be leaving Chackmore Manor. It would be easier to imagine the house pulling away from its own foundations and walking down the High Street. He would calm his wife down and find out what was really happening.

'Cup of tea?'

'Look, listen to me,' responded his wife. 'I know exactly what you're thinking, and no, I've *not* got it wrong. It's true – they actually *are* leaving!'

Mr Thompson realised that he was going to have to take this more seriously. 'And the evidence is?'

'I bumped into Lady Harrison-Smythe in the Post Office, and she told me . . . came straight out with it, absolutely streaming with tears.'

This did sound like good evidence. 'But they can't. It's not possible.'

'I know that,' said his wife impatiently, 'but they are – *today* – at this very moment!'

Mr Thompson at last heaved himself off the sofa and swung into action. 'Charlie!' he shouted upstairs. 'Come on, we're going for a walk!'

En route, he explained to his younger son trotting beside him, just why it was so inconceivable that the H-S's should be leaving Chackmore Manor. 'They've been there for generations, since before the Conquest. They can trace their family tree and possession of the Manor right back to Wellbred the Proud of Mercia – and there are possible links with the legendary Nevahaere the Absent of Wessex, and even Unraede the Illiterate.' Charlie was concentrating hard and trying to find this fascinating. 'And the church in the grounds

– stuffed full of their family's monuments! The finest alabaster tombs in the county. They *can't* leave – Lord H-S once told me the only way he was leaving the Manor was to be carried out in a box.'

They rounded the final corner and came within sight of the wrought-iron entrance gates. The road in front was virtually blocked by a long line of removal lorries, most of them in the final stages of the job, with men slamming the large doors at the side and rear of the vehicles. Beyond the final lorry stood Lord and Lady Harrison-Smythe, she with her head on his shoulders, he holding her close to comfort her, both looking shell-shocked. Mr Thompson didn't feel it was right to intrude. He turned slowly around and the two began to wander sadly back to their house.

Down a side lane, Charlie spotted a large black car parked below an overhanging tree, its engine calmly ticking over, as if waiting to move. It was the smartest car he'd seen in the village for a long time, a brand-new Bentley no less, and he was dead impressed by the smart uniformed chauffeur behind the wheel. Charlie would have been equally impressed if he'd seen the dominating and powerful figure sat in the rear, but not if he'd heard his quiet words.

'They've all got their guilty secrets,' the passenger was muttering to himself. 'Especially our dear respected landed gentry. Works every time. Just a little anonymous card – *flee at once, all is discovered*. Pathetically easy.' He leaned forward, slid open the small glass partition, and gave the clipped instructions. 'Past the Manor – *very* slowly.' The car began to ease down the lane. 'This,' whispered the passenger, 'is a moment to treasure.'

Jedekiah Biddle, the new Lord of the Manor of Chackmore, was pleased with himself. The new plan was coming together nicely, very nicely indeed.

2 : New Tasks

'It's a real honour to be given a tour of the archives, especially by the Permanent Grand Archivist.' Jamie was talking into his sleeve again as they approached the old porch doors of the parish church at Malplaquet.

'Indeed it is, sir, but your size does prevent a full tour of the facilities. Nevertheless, you will be able to peer into the main entrance, and then allow your imagination to wander around the innermost recesses. Do close these church doors as well – they warn us of approaching humans.'

Jamie closed them behind him and gently stepped into the cool interior, its ancient walls painted a crisp sky-blue. He knew the building from the occasional Carol Service and a couple of Christenings. 'I never realised there was a collection of old documents here,' he whispered to Nigriff, setting him down on the stone floor under the rear organ gallery. 'Isn't it a bit odd, using a church?'

'Master Jamie,' replied Nigriff, with an air of surprise, 'it is the *logical* setting for items of such value. This is the only building guaranteed to remain untouched by the passing whims of architects, heritage advisers, and garden designers. When the surrounding village was swept away by the first dukes, it stood as an unmoveable and timeless rock, and it will continue to do so.'

Fair enough, thought Jamie.

'Furthermore,' continued Nigriff, 'it is one of the few outlying buildings that has its own heating system, an incomparable and essential benefit to the preservation of our papers. And where else would one keep one's most holy objects?'

'Okay, I get the point,' agreed Jamie. 'So exactly where in here are the archives?'

'If you would position yourself on the floor by that heating vent, I will be with you in a moment.' With that, Nigriff strode briskly off past a pew.

Jamie knelt down by the wall and peered through the patterned metal grille into what seemed to be a completely dark void. An instant later the space was flooded with light, and Jamie saw Nigriff striding towards a small desk about twenty centimetres away. Behind it lay a central walkway, with rows of shelving, drawers and racks extending on either side. Tiny rolls were protruding from some open compartments. At the far end of the main aisle were two tables with minuscule books and sheets of paper spread across them. It was all very neat and purposeful.

Nigriff firmly tapped a domed brass bell on the desk and wandered back to the grille to speak to Jamie.

'The timing of your visit is *perfect*, young sir, as by a happy coincidence today sees the trial of a new system. Normally, I would walk in and collect the relevant document, but the Directors are implementing a procedure that is very common – and therefore presumably *much* admired – in your world. Apparently it increases efficiency, and the transmission of information. The operator will appear soon.'

'Sounds good, Nigriff. I'll just lie here and watch.'

Nigriff walked back, and pressed the bell again. Thirkatew, a young female Lilliputian, appeared from one side. She stopped at the other side of the desk, stared him straight in the face, and spoke in a cheery and bubbly voice.

'Thank you for calling at the Archives. You are advised that your call may be monitored for training purposes. Please choose one of the following options. Press once for archives, twice for ancient documents, three times for old writings, or four to speak to the Operator.'

Nigriff turned to look happily at Jamie, winked as if to say, 'Good, isn't it?' and pushed the bell deliberately four times.

The young girl remained impassive, staring directly ahead and saying nothing. This seemed to slightly unsettle Nigriff. He raised his hand to strike the bell again, but Thirkatew suddenly said, 'All our operators are currently busy. Please hold.' With that, she stepped back, sat down, took out a type of recorder or flute from her pocket, and began to play a tune – which Jamie vaguely recognised as a symphonic piece that required a full orchestra and more musical talent than was currently evident.

Nigriff, much bemused, turned back to look quizzically at Jamie. 'Try again,' came the suggestion. Nigriff thumped the bell four times. It had the desired effect. The recorder playing stopped; Thirkatew got to her feet, and looked at Nigriff. Then she pronounced, as cheerfully as before, 'Your call is very important to us. Please continue to hold.' With that she resumed her seat, found her recorder, and began again, right from the very first bar.

Nigriff walked back to Jamie, who tried to be helpful. 'Teething problems?'

'I'm not sure . . . Perhaps it was my mistake to contact the Operator at the start. I'll try again.' He walked away as if he was leaving the archives. Thirkatew stopped inflicting pain on the recorder and stood up to leave her position.

Nigriff, however, turned smartly on his heels, approached the desk, and banged the bell. The Operator stared at him (rather coldly, Jamie thought), and repeated, 'Thank you for calling the Archives. You are advised that your call may . . .' Before she could finish, Nigriff thumped the bell twice, very hard. She stopped in mid-flow, thought for a moment, and then declared, 'All lines to Ancient Documents are busy at the moment. Your call is held in a queue, and will be answered in approximately . . . ,' and she paused, as if thinking of a number, 'six minutes.' The recorder reappeared from her pocket. Only one note was emitted before it was drowned by another strident noise – Nigriff, doing something that Jamie had never seen before. He was shouting.

'What in the name of Rentur the Mighty do you mean my call is held in a queue? There's no-one else *here*! *What* queue?'

Any normal person would have been flustered by his words and manner, but Thirkatew's calm and measured reply revealed her excellent training. 'We are currently experiencing a sudden increase in call volume. Please continue to hold, or try again later. Your call is important to us, and . . . .'

'I think I'd like to *hold*,' declared Nigriff firmly, and he grabbed the recorder from the girl's hands, put it across his knee and snapped it in half. Then he strode round past the desk, disappeared behind some shelves, and rapidly re-emerged clutching a large roll of paper. He took one last look at the bell on the desk, picked it up, dropped it on the floor and stamped on it hard. It emitted one dull note as it gave way beneath his feet. The unflappable Thirkatew began, 'Thank you for calling . . . .'

Nigriff swiftly interrupted her. 'Do not even *think* about it, young lady,' he snarled, and marched out.

Jamie was waiting for him at the rear of the church. Nigriff was still fuming. 'I do not wish to discuss this incident, Master Jamie. My outburst is highly regrettable. I will be speaking to the Directors; there must be a fault in the system.'

'You're probably right,' said Jamie. 'It can't be meant to work like that. But you got what you wanted?'

'Indeed, I am glad to say. Allow me to unroll this remarkable map.' He spread it out on the ground. 'It was drawn by some of the original kidnapped victims in the early days of our residence at Maplaquet, probably as a wistful reminder of their homeland.'

Fortunately the map had been drawn on a very large sheet of Lilliputian paper, so Jamie could read some of the bigger words by squinting hard. They both let their eyes wander over its outline and detail.

After a couple of minutes, they sat back and looked at each other. Without a word, Nigriff rolled up the document, Jamie carefully placed him with the map in an inside pocket, and they hurried out the door.

John Biddle, the only child of the new owner of Chackmore Manor, picked his way through the tangled piles of lead piping, brass handles and wooden panelling that were scattered around the entrance hall. His new home was reverberating to banging and thumping and drilling. He looked up at the winding carved oak staircase, as four workmen tried to manoeuvre a huge old bath with clawed feet round the top corner. Another careless shove cut a deep gouge into the polished wood of the newel-post, snapping off part of a carving of

Adam and Eve. 'Careful, you've just committed the first sin,' said one of the men in mock concern. 'It's not *his* first sin!' laughed one of the others. 'Come on, pass me the hammer – we'll smash it here.'

As the resonant clanging started, John wandered through the front double doors, and shielded his eyes to look at the view. Past the workers' vans and lorries he could see a couple of small lakes, with a rowing-boat tied to the bank of one, and sheep grazing in the gently-sloping fields beyond. He looked to his left, past the new conservatory already being constructed, to the ancient brick-built church on the end of the line of buildings. Horses stood in the fields behind, occasionally looking up at all the noise and hubbub.

John wasn't sure what to think about this place. He knew he could be happy here – he knew he *ought* to be happy here – but the move had been so sudden and unexpected. He was now missing his one friend, and he wasn't much good at making new ones. Why was the move necessary? Did his father know how he felt?

He was lost in these thoughts when a man, whom he recognised as a business friend of his father, marched over and without a word thrust a bright yellow envelope into John's hands. He looked at the typed words – *Master J. Biddle, Esquire*. It was from his father. That much was obvious.

John felt pleased that he had this letter directly from him. An earlier note written by one of the workers had simply read, '*Mr Biddle regrets that current work commitments do not allow him to join you at the Manor for the foreseeable future.*' John hated any messages from them, so it was good to have one written by his Dad himself. But it would have been better if he'd actually been here.

John opened it slowly, not wanting to hurry or damage the best link he had with his father at present. He folded back the yellow sheet.

John,
You will by now be enjoying the Manor. It needs improving, but when I have got rid of the old stuff it will be a useful base. I have instructed the men to convert the Music room into a Cinema, and I will buy you a Quad-bike soon.
I know it is difficult to make friends – you didn't have any before – and it's one of your failings we will in time correct. I have taken the trouble to find out about local families, and there

*is one boy that you must get to know. He is Charles Thompson,
and he lives in the High Street with his parents and older brother.
He is slightly younger than you, which makes it easier for you
to get to know him. His brother Jamie is a difficult character;
have nothing to do with him for the moment. Charles likes going
out on his bike; slowly ride down the street on yours and he will
spot you.*

*If you are worried about starting at the new school, think how
many others you have attended. You are used to it; it will not be
a problem. Schools all study the same subjects anyway. At this
one, you must work extremely hard at Visual Education; it will
help you become an architect if you are capable of doing so.*

JB

John read the letter again, noting the parts where his father seemed
concerned, such as trying to help him make friends, or thinking
about his future career.

'Come on, kid, move out of the way!' A loud and grunting voice
startled him, and he leapt back out of the doorway. A large wooden
crate, about one metre square and covered in stickers saying, 'Fragile'
or 'This Way Up,' was being wheeled in on a trolley by four men.
'Put it in the study, and make sure all the window locks are fitted.
Bring me the keys straight after.' The instructions came from a fierce
man with a walking-stick. John knew it was time to be scarce. He
went to see if his bike had been left anywhere.

Charlie was in a snooping mood and was wandering around the
house whilst the other three were out. The summer holidays were
nearly over, which was a pain, but they had been good fun. He had
some stories to laugh about with his friends, and he'd been taken on
a couple of stimulating family trips, doubtless cunningly planned
by his parents to impress any teacher who set the essay, *What I did
this Summer*. Mr and Mrs Thompson had not yet forgotten their
embarrassment when Charlie hadn't warned them about his Food
Technology project. He had faithfully kept a detailed record, down
to the very last baked bean and oven-ready chip, of their week's
menus and food intake.

Anyway, Charlie was now happily snooping, mainly in Jamie's

stuff; he knew his brother well, and Jamie was *definitely* behaving oddly. It might be because he'd turned thirteen and was starting a new school, but Charlie was sure there was something else. Jamie had become far too interested in old buildings and gardens, never mind the poetry that his Mum was worried about, written by some pope or other.

He tried the usual hiding places – in the sock drawer, under the corner of the carpet, and inside the old wooden box right at the back of the high cupboard. He even managed to access his brother's new laptop and found a file marked *Nothing Special*, which led to *Not Worth Looking In,* and wisely decided that Jamie was obviously laying false trails. He sat down cross-legged on the floor, with a nagging feeling that he had missed something. He looked around the room again.

Of course! Below the bed . . . the first place in any emergency. Charlie squirmed under the outer edge, probing carefully everywhere with his fingers. Out came two socks, a tennis ball, screwed-up bits of paper, an empty Mars Bar wrapper, a footballer card, and a large red book. 'Very incriminating,' thought Charlie. 'So that's where my chocolate went.'

He idly allowed the book to fall open at the inside front cover. It was a drawing of a large garden full of woods, lakes, and unusual buildings, and it was called *The Palace of Malplaquet.* Charlie recognised the huge arch, an obelisk, a tall pillar, and the mansion, though not quite as he remembered them. He also spotted a signature, in what he reckoned was a young female hand. It was simply, *Maria.*

'Yes!' exclaimed Charlie. 'That's it – the boy's in *love*! This is *very* promising. . . .' He jumped to his feet and began making connections. 'She's probably local, often visits the gardens, knows a lot about them like girls do . . . So Jamie has to impress her by learning all this stuff, even old poetry . . . Yes, it all makes sense . . . he asks to borrow her books . . .'

He stopped in mid-deduction by the window. Outside he'd noticed a boy, perhaps older than him, pedalling slowly and shakily down the road. The boy was interesting, because Charlie hadn't seen him before, but it was the smart bike that really gripped his attention. Titanium everywhere, elliptical cross-section minimal spokes, semi-automatic gear change, no-grease 'technosport' chain, heated saddle . . . it had the lot.

'Good grief!' Charlie exclaimed. 'A Revelation, in Chackmore!' He dropped the book, ran out of the room, ran back in again, threw the book under the bed, and jumped down the stairs. 'That,' he said to himself, 'is a bike – I mean, a boy – worth getting to know.' He jogged out to meet him.

Nigriff and Jamie were separately searching everywhere for Granny, having agreed to meet back at her cottage in an hour. The archivist had been scouring Palladia, and, finding himself by the Pebble Alcove, had decided to do some research on it and thus 'kill two birds with one stone' (a phrase disliked by the local Palladians, who had a close relationship with the birds, even understanding their whistles). So he was now standing inside the niche, staring high above him at the collection of pebbly squiggles and patterns pressed into its walls, and feeling foolish. He simply didn't know what to do. Jamie, who had seen more Gulliver images than anybody else, had told him to, 'Just let your eyes drift around the shapes until one catches your attention, then stare at it.' It sounded an extremely random and unreliable method to a trained archivist like Nigriff, but with little alternative he did exactly that.

Within seconds his eyes were attracted to the outline of a pair of glasses. He fixed his gaze on them. Instantly a grey mist slipped down across the entrance and, because this was exactly what Jamie had said might happen, Nigriff was slightly relieved. An image appeared on this screen, again just as Jamie had predicted. This was of a giant man, dressed in a long jacket. One of the outer pockets had two small heads poking out of it.

Nigriff knew immediately that this was Gulliver. 'It was when he was being searched, just after he'd been brought to Mildendo,' he thought. Once the Lilliputians had finished and been placed back on the ground, Gulliver gently patted a slight bulge on the inside of his coat without anyone noticing. 'They missed the secret pocket for his telescope and glasses,' mused Nigriff.

Gulliver then poured a small amount of black powder into a pistol, pointed the gun into the air and pulled the trigger. The explosion was terrific, and immediately blew apart the Alcove's screen and image. As the mist dispersed, Nigriff caught a brief and fading glimpse of hundreds of Lilliputians running away. 'Jamie has said that these pictures are like *clues*, telling us something,' he pondered. 'Maybe I should be hiding things . . . or using a gun . . . most strange.'

He plodded out, muttering to himself, '*Words* are always better than pictures, far better. Now, where in this world is the dear lady?'

Inside a small marquee, the Estate Volunteers' Team Leader at Malplaquet was addressing his new group. A broad-shouldered man with a well-tanned face and a mass of curly hair, he was trying to put at ease the new people seated in front of him.

'First of all, on behalf of all of the inhabitants of Malplaquet – the animals, as well as the people . . . and the trees, because they're important . . . you can talk to them, even the shrubs. Like the Elder, you should always respect your elders, ha ha, just my little joke – can I say welcome?'

Vicky looked around at the other volunteers. They were a mixed bag. Amongst them were a handful of people her age, perhaps one or two taking a Gap Year, a middle-aged woman attentively hanging on the leader's every word, some older men who were probably just retired, and one particularly weather-beaten man with a craggy face and long side-whiskers. He was also wearing a floppy hat, which made it difficult to get a really good look at him.

The man warbled on and on, and Vicky half-dozed her way through his presentation; she already knew, from her previous work at weekends, much of what was involved.

' . . . So that's settled, we'll have the girls working on the plants for a few weeks, while the boys get stuck into the wall, I don't mean that literally like, it's the stones we want in it, ha ha . . . actually it *is* called a ha-ha, that's even funnier, ha ha. I actually *was* laughing then, not telling you about the wall, the ha-ha . . .' Vicky made a rapid decision and approached the Volunteers' Leader as they all left the marquee.

'Excuse me, I don't want to cause any trouble, but can I work on the wall instead, you know, the ha-ha?'

'But – not being funny or anything – you're a girl, aren't you?'

'Yes, obviously . . . but that doesn't mean I have to like flowers. I prefer building work – I've often helped my Dad with bricklaying and stuff.'

He scratched his head. The concept of a female doing fairly heavy manual labour was causing him some difficulty. 'Well, I don't know, I suppose we could give it a try . . . summat unusual like, that might bring in more visitors . . .' He reluctantly agreed, and Vicky trudged off with the men towards the trailer, with its wheelbarrows, spades, and bags of sand and cement.

She knew that she had just made herself the object of attention, but her task – as agreed with Jamie and Granny – was to try to keep an eye on all those who were working in the gardens. No-one knew how, when or with whom their enemy might strike next.

As Nigriff had said, 'We must try to anticipate Biddle's every move.'

Or as Thorclan had said, 'I expect we cannot expect the unexpected. That's only to be expected.'

Either way, it was not going to be an easy year.

3: Ties of Friendship

'This is no good – she could be anywhere,' groaned Jamie. As arranged, he and Nigriff had met back at Granny's cottage, to find the door still locked and the windows shut.

'I confess that you are right, sir. It is sometimes extremely hard to locate her in grounds of this magnitude. Should we consider hiring a squirrel? I could whistle for one – the Palladian Chillkin has kindly been teaching me some of the finer points of his technique.'

At any other time Jamie would have remarked upon Nigriff's increasing friendship with his fellow Lilliputians, but he was too flustered at that moment. 'No, not now. Maybe I can hot-wire her electric buggy.'

'There are two difficulties with that proposal, sir. Firstly, we do not have a hot wire. Secondly, one observes that the doors of the shed are open, with wet tyre tracks emerging from the permanent puddle by its entrance. I can only assume that the splendid machine and its owner are both absent, and probably together.'

Nigriff barely finished speaking before Jamie had shot off in a cloud of dust. The little man immediately stuck two fingers in his mouth, inhaled deeply, and produced a high-pitched sonic wave of such intensity, frequency and appeal that all dog-walkers within three miles were suddenly pulled in its direction by their frantic hounds. It worked on Jamie as well. He jogged back, shame-faced and panting. 'Sorry – too excited. Smart whistle though.'

'No more than a Chillkin special. However, it has left me slightly breathless. A lift would be much appreciated.' He was picked up, still clutching the precious map from the Archives, and dropped carefully into Jamie's top pocket.

It was easy to follow the tyre tracks along the perimeter walk to the Temple of Friendship, where they quickly spotted the old lady on the grass below the old ruin. Seated on her tartan rug by her buggy (or *GT* as Jamie called it, short for 'Golf Trolley'), she was facing the river and the open view towards the Palladian Bridge and Gothic Temple. Fiddling with her dressmaking equipment and materials, and deep in concentration, she was surprised when Jamie suddenly appeared from behind.

'Goodness, you made me jump! I wasn't expecting to see you today, Jamie. Are you by yourself?'

'No, I've got Nigriff as well,' puffed Jamie.

'Only by good fortune, Madam,' came the sharp comment from the little figure, poking his head out. 'I had to ensure that we had a whistle-stop tour.'

Granny smiled. 'Well, it's such a lovely day I thought I'd work outside.' She patted the rug. 'Come and sit down – and what have you been up to, getting all hot and flustered?'

'Something really exciting,' said Jamie, settling down. 'From the Archives.'

'Oh yes, Nigriff, you were telling me about a new system . . .'

'Disconnected,' said Nigriff tersely. 'Customer satisfaction levels.'

'Anyway,' said Jamie rapidly, 'Nigriff found this, an old map of Lilliput.' It was unrolled, about the size of a small envelope, and passed to Granny, who squinted closely at it. 'It's very hard to read,' she said.

Nigriff suddenly remembered the images he had seen in the Pebble Alcove. 'Can I recommend spectacles?' he remarked. So that was why he had been shown those particular scenes. The building *was* sending helpful messages, as Jamie had been claiming.

'You're absolutely right, Nigriff,' agreed Granny. 'Lucky I've got my strongest dressmaking ones with me.' She rummaged in her bag, found the case, and put on her glasses, which made a substantial difference. 'Hmm,' she murmured. 'It's beautifully drawn. And still wonderfully clear after so long. There's Mildendo, the capital, or the 'metropolis' as Gulliver called it . . . and one or two rivers . . . and all sorts of other regions.'

'Can you read any, Granny? Look at the one to the right of the city.'

She peered more steadily. '*Imperial barracks and parade ground*,' she read.

'And the collection of buildings just below it?' suggested Jamie again.

'I can just make out *schools . . . nurseries . . . library*.'

'Now – imagine that this area isn't *Lilliput*, but *Malplaquet*.' Granny nodded silently. 'Mildendo matches the mansion. Who's living in the area marked *barracks*?'

'The Grecians,' she whispered slowly, not taking her eyes off the map.

'And in the places of learning, the *schools*?'

'The Elysians . . ,' she murmured slowly. 'And look,' she gabbled, pointing to one corner of the island, '*workshops, factories and foundries* – in Palladia. I can't quite read the other bit . . . the writing's too small.'

'*Physical recreation and diversions*,' added Nigriff. 'Cascadia, if you will.'

There was a moment of silence as all three let the idea sink in. There could be no doubt about it. Jamie had previously been suggesting that the outline of Malplaquet and the island of Lilliput did seem to be remarkably similar, but now the three friends had realised something else. It was frankly extraordinary; the types of buildings on the original island of Lilliput matched absolutely perfectly with the character of the four provinces and their inhabitants at Malplaquet. There was no denying it.

'What an amazing coincidence,' uttered Granny, quite shocked.

'It *can't* be just coincidence,' answered Jamie immediately. 'The odds are astronomical.'

'So how do you explain it? Nigriff, is there anything in the Archives?'

'I can confidently say almost *certainly*, Madam, but non-domesticated equine quadrupeds would not entice me there at present.' Jamie translated it for Granny's benefit to 'wild horses wouldn't drag him.'

'So where does that leave us?' she asked.

'With another puzzle,' said Jamie, 'but also another answer. It's totally confirmed what we thought about "The capital gained." It's definitely the mansion.'

'This discovery may enrich my talk to the Academic Board tomorrow,' said Nigriff. 'I can now put some finishing touches to my speech.'

'Wait a minute,' said Granny. 'I've just thought. If Malplaquet really is like Lilliput, shouldn't we expect to find another island? You know, the one that Gulliver waded out to, and captured their fleet of ships?'

'Blefuscu,' added Nigriff, 'hostile Empire to Lilliput, home of the exiles in the Big-Endian egg controversy. If my memory is correct, it was roughly eight hundred of your yards away, on the opposite side of the island from Mildendo. Therefore, if we are to confirm our theory, a military construction exists in that direction.' He pointed back up the slope past the Temple of Friendship. 'We should investigate.'

'There's not much out there,' said Jamie. 'Just open fields and farmland.'

They nonetheless wandered back up towards Friendship. At the top of the rise, behind the ruin and standing above the ha-ha, they shielded their eyes against the sun and looked out across the acres of stubble.

In profound silence, they all noticed the solitary building.

An old farmhouse could be seen roughly half a mile away, with very long and high walls. Walls with turrets and castellations. Looking exactly like a fort.

'Blimey,' said Jamie.

'Blefuscu,' said Nigriff.

'Blow me down,' said Granny. 'I'd forgotten about that place.'

'When did they do that?' asked Jamie.

'In the eighteenth century,' replied Granny. 'Oh dear, this is beginning to get awfully complicated.'

Over the course of two days Charlie had come to realise that he had probably missed a trick with that book under Jamie's bed. If it *had* been given to his brother by his new girl-friend Maria – and that was the most obvious explanation for the signature and Jamie's erratic behaviour – there might be a little note or scribbled message inside its pages. The sort of things that girls wrote, like 'missing you lots,' or 'I really want to see you xxx.' Charlie himself had never received one, but he'd seen girls write them in lessons, so he'd decided it was his family duty to discover if Jamie had any.

So he was now sat on the floor in his brother's bedroom, leafing through the book entitled, *Mistress Masham's Repose*.

He was disgruntled not to find a single piece of endearing and incriminating evidence. In one sense he was pleased – 'she obviously doesn't fancy him *that* much,' he thought – but he was also disappointed. The opportunity to set up a few embarrassing scenarios at the family dinner-table was not yet presenting itself. The evidence, though solid, might backfire; Jamie was bound to deny it all ('she's just one of my friends'), and Charlie would only be able to back up his own deductions with a signature in a book. He needed more.

As he quickly flipped through the volume, occasionally shaking it upside-down in case he missed the notes, the pictures caught his eye, and he realised that it was a children's story about little people who lived in Malplaquet's gardens. There were also humans, such as an old woman with her hair tied up in a bun, a cross-looking vicar, a fat policeman, and a young girl with glasses and pig-tails. 'It's like *Gulliver's Travels*,' he thought, remembering the book he'd once dipped into at Granny's. He slid it back under the bed, and was just thinking about where to look next, when his Mum shouted upstairs.

'Charlie, that new boy John is outside the front again.'

Quietly sneaking out of Jamie's bedroom, carefully avoiding the creaky floorboard, he answered from the safety of his own doorway. 'With his bike?'

'Yes. Why don't you go out and play with him?'

Charlie always hated it when his Mum said things like that, but the lure of that bike got the better of him. He thumped downstairs and ran outside.

Vicky was beginning to wonder whether she had made the right decision. It wasn't that she was finding the work hard – she was used to getting her hands dirty, and it was good to be physically active after a lazy summer – but the chaps in her work-party were such a dull lot. None of them seemed interested in getting to know her; in fact, she felt they resented her intrusion on their scene. Conversation had proven extremely difficult. She had eventually found out that one was called Ralph and he had lived 'around here' for some time. Two or three were definitely avoiding her, and another member of the team was so shy as to be unreal – all he had been able to do was to say to her was, 'Really?' or, in his more confident moments, 'I know what you mean.' Perhaps he wanted to keep himself to himself.

She parked her rusty and squeaking wheelbarrow near the pile of old stones that had been left on the corner of the ha-ha. Her job was to find the ones with the flattest edges to be used in the face of the wall. Spotting a suitable lump, she bent down, grabbed the stone in both gloved hands – and then leapt back, emitting a small shriek, and dropping the weight on the grass.

'Good morning, Miss Vicky,' said Yenech cheerily, crawling out from amongst the rocks.

'Mornin' Miss,' agreed Wesel, poking his head out suddenly from one side, catching her off-guard again.

'Hi ya!' shouted Hyroc from the stone right by her feet, provoking another squeal from Vicky and an instinctive jump back.

'Don't *do* that!' she gasped. 'It's not funny.' She stared at all three in turn. 'And that's not a very safe place to hide.'

They all looked suitably crestfallen. 'We're not hiding,' said Yenech, 'we're in *training*. This is our limestone crags section.'

'Well, all I can say is make the most of them, because these hills won't be here forever; in fact, they'll be gone by the end of the week. And what are you training for?'

'Who knows?' replied Yenech. 'But there'll always be a need for the Thompson Quad Squad. Any crisis or difficulties, TQS are always on hand and underfoot. We've got a motto now, haven't we, chaps?'

Wesel and Hyroc nodded. They stood either side of Yenech, shoulders together, arms folded, and said loudly and firmly in unison, 'TQS, the dream team – your problem . . . is *us*.'

'Right,' said Vicky. 'I see what you mean. Just, um, wait for the call, won't you? And keep away from anything that might be picked up in a digger or wheelbarrow. There's some dangerous stuff for little people round here.'

'Don't worry, Miss Vicky, we'll keep our eyes open. By the way, who are all these men you're working with? Can we trust them?'

'I'm not sure. That's why I wanted to hang around. I've got a funny feeling about one or two.'

'If you've got a funny feeling, then so have I,' insisted Yenech. 'Men, this sounds like another mission. Synchronise watches.'

'Yenech, this really isn't necessary . . . .'

'No need to worry, Miss Vicky. Everyone ready? Let's go!'

'But Yenech . . . where are you going?' shouted Vicky at the departing figures.

'Couldn't possibly tell you,' came the faint reply, as they disappeared into the twitching undergrowth.

No change there, thought Vicky.

John Biddle was nervous about a friend coming back home. He himself hadn't suggested it of course, but he'd been so shocked when Charlie had said, 'Can we go to your house?' that he'd simply nodded. No-one had asked him that for ages. His father had always decided which local children were not 'suitable,' which was usually most of them, so it wasn't surprising that John rarely brought any school-friends back.

'The Manor's fun,' Charlie had said *en route*, 'I've been there loads of times. Village fêtes, fireworks that sort of thing.'

'Sounds really good,' had been John's reply.

As they reached the Manor, Charlie realised why he'd been smelling smoke all morning. The gates were swung back to reveal a scene of utter devastation. Down the long drive were several large bonfires, crackling away through the charred and blackened remains of doors and window shutters. Men were dragging bundles of planks and floorboards, and old boxes and cupboards were being tossed on the flames.

'They said the place was full of woodworm, and weevils and stuff,' said John. Charlie felt sad. He looked across to one of the nearby lawns, where a digger was scraping away the top layer of grass and earth, and piling it into a lorry. It had been one of the finest croquet lawns in the country, Charlie remembered. Lady Harrison-Smythe had always insisted on the players bringing their own slippers.

John noticed his gaze. 'I think it's a heli-pad,' he said.

'What about over there?' asked Charlie, looking towards the brick-walled kitchen garden into which a crane was dropping some large green corrugated sheets. 'They're building a laboratory for my father's research,' came the proud reply. 'He's very clever.'

The main entrance-hall was very different from when Charlie had last seen it, at the village Summer Fête in July. Gone was the polished and creaky wood, the tapestry with its scene of a royal pageant, the central chandelier that Lord H-S had bought in an auction in Paris, the portraits on the stairs, the smell of dogs and fields. Instead there were hard cold surfaces – imitation pine flooring, yellow boarding right up to the ceilings where the cornices used to be, noticeboards, a series of pigeonholes, and silvery metal lamps standing in corners by bright green potted plants.

On the wall facing the boys was a large portrait lit from above. It showed a proud gentleman standing in front of a naval scene. He was wearing a tightly-curled wig, a heavily-embroidered jacket with enormous cuffs, and held a telescope wedged under his left arm. He was looking down at a map in his right hand.

'He's our really famous ancestor,' said John proudly. 'Captain John Biddle. I'm named after him.'

'I've got to lick you two into shape, so I'm going to give you a flavour of winter exercises,' announced Yenech to Wesel and Hyroc. 'Starting with the use of the ropes and grappling-hook; very useful in steep snow-covered terrain.'

They were standing behind the trunk of a fallen tree at the edge of the car park. The nearest vehicles were thirty yards away, so they were safe from prying eyes.

'The crucial point is to make sure that when you throw the hook, it attaches to something firm.' Yenech hurled the end of the rope over the top of the log. It did attach itself to something firm, the base of an ice-cream cone held by a toddler seated on the other side. The boy didn't see the hook sink in, but he felt a slight movement and looked at his treat quizzically, touching the chocolate flake.

'Now give the rope a firm pull to make sure that it's solid. Ninety-nine times out of a hundred it's fine.' Yenech leaned back and gave it a powerful yank – strong enough to snatch the ice-cream from the boy's grasp and loop it high into the air. Yenech felt the rope go slack. 'Well, this isn't one of those ninety-nines,' he said.

'Yes, it is!' shouted Wesel, looking up at the incoming missile. 'Avalanche!'

Only a split-second later Yenech was encased in a snow-white mound of Mr. Wispee's 'Summer's Best.' By a stroke of good fortune, the flake had become detached during the flight and it landed a few inches away, breaking up on impact and showering Wesel and Hyroc in chocolate splinters. It was their lucky day.

The parents of the young boy had seen him fling his ice-cream over his shoulder, and the father had swiftly run over and picked up the child. 'No, you can't go and get it! It'll have all sorts of nasty things in it!' The toddler had been carried off kicking and screaming, never to forget the day when his ice-cream had made a successful bid for freedom.

Wesel and Hyroc were enjoying the sudden end to their day's training. Biting on yet another chocolate sliver, and watching Yenech clear his eyes to improve visibility, they knew that the next stage was the review of the task.

'You know you wanted to lick us into shape,' queried Wesel. 'Can we do the same for you?'

'And this "flavour of winter exercises" you mentioned,' added Hyroc. 'Exactly what flavour is it? Vanilla – or a hint of mint?'

Yenech scooped away a large dollop from under his chin. 'This,' he assured them, 'is the sweet taste of success. Tuck in, my good men; the food's on me.'

John Biddle was initially excited to be handed another note from his father. It was unusual to receive two in quick succession. But as he opened it, he suddenly wondered if it meant he'd done something wrong, which made him anxious as he began to read. Fortunately some words sounded positive.

John,

I gather you have met with the younger Thompson boy on two occasions now. That is the correct way to proceed, as I instructed you. Bear in mind what I said about keeping away from his brother at present. A time may come when I tell you to make contact with him, but not yet.

When you start at Malplaquet School, remember my words about the Visual Education lessons. I have no interest in your performance in other subjects; one can become powerful without reading old books or studying obscure languages and facts. Ordinary people can be paid to do tedious work; we leaders must be free from mundane tasks.

John stopped to think. There was no doubt that his father was a clever and successful man. Just look at this house he was living in and all these people running around doing what he wanted. He returned to the letter.

The Visual Education course will teach you about the grounds and buildings – it will open your eyes, reveal wonderful and extraordinary things, astonishing and valuable sights that mortals have rarely seen. Too much about Malplaquet has remained hidden, even to me. But now, together, we will uncover some of its deepest secrets, its remarkable treasures, the Biddle destiny that has for centuries been denied us . . . . The time has at last arrived! This will be our proudest moment!

Signed, as ever,
JB

This last paragraph unsettled John. Partly because he didn't have the faintest idea what his father was on about, but also the tone of it was different. His father sounded too determined, agitated, vengeful perhaps. From what John knew of him, he had always got his own way, but usually he was measured and steady, like an irresistible tide gradually sliding up a beach and swallowing everything in its path. But now his father seemed more like a storm out at sea, stirring up huge waves and ready to crash on an unsuspecting shore.

John shook himself, surprised by the clarity of this image. He looked up at the portrait of his namesake above him. All these ideas about the coast and storms and things. Perhaps it was in the family blood. Whatever it was, he decided there and then that he was going to work really hard at this Visual Education; he didn't want to either let his father down or, more importantly, disobey him.

4 : Origins and Beginnings

'There's only one problem,' said Jamie. 'We've no idea what we're doing.'

'Splendid,' enthused Thorclan. 'Exactly what the Grecian army is used to. This is our speciality.'

Granny and Jamie exchanged worried glances. They were finalising their plan for 'gaining the capital,' as Pope's poem had prophecied. In fact, *finalising* was a rather optimistic word; actually *having* a plan was their first task.

'So far we think we have to invade the mansion – the capital,' said Jamie. 'Which sounds a bit weird . . . Has Nigriff had any good ideas yet?'

'Not really,' said Granny. 'It's a pity he's not here, but he's completing his research for his talk tonight to the Academic Board.'

'The academic *bored*?' grunted Thorclan. 'That's no surprise.'

'The thing that he *does* keep mentioning,' offered Granny, 'is that all these buildings, like the Pebble Alcove, have got special forces in them . . .'

'And the mansion will soon have *my* Special Forces in it,' interrupted Thorclan.

'Not those sort, Nigriff means something different,' responded Granny. 'A type of energy, or power perhaps.'

'Got it! The man's a genius,' exclaimed Thorclan. 'Should have seen it myself. Sir, Madam, leave it to me. I know where the power is; both of the heating boilers are located in basement rooms in the West Wing. I'll take a handpicked team of crack commandos, attach a couple of charges, lay out the wiring . . .'

'General, blowing up the central heating and cutting off their hot water won't help,' said Granny.

'No, of course, you're right,' agreed Thorclan. 'It might even toughen the blighters up. Far too soft they are nowadays. I remember, back in the Bourbon conflict, my men and I lived off our *sweat* for weeks. Even had baths in it; the enemy ran a mile when they smelt us coming.'

'Any ideas about how we could empty the building?' asked Granny.

'Set off the fire alarms?' said Jamie. 'But the people would soon come back in again anyway, I suppose.'

'Cut off their food supplies,' said Thorclan. 'But it might toughen the blighters up. Far too soft they are nowadays. I remember, back in the Dadford conflict . . . .'

'This isn't getting us anywhere,' said Granny. 'We need to think laterally, outside the box, with different coloured hats on, some blue sky thinking.' At least that silenced Thorclan; he hadn't a clue what she was on about. It took a while to explain that they just wanted some more imaginative ideas.

They knew they couldn't possibly invade the whole mansion, so they would have to strike at its very heart, at something that was *vital* or *central* to the building. What could that be?

Thorclan knew the answer straightaway.

'Our mission is clear,' he replied confidently. 'I know what's *central*. It's in the centre – the Marble Saloon. I believe it's called that because it's marble and it was once a saloon.'

'You think we should go there?' said Jamie. 'Are you sure?'

Thorclan nodded.

'It's our best, well, our *only* suggestion at the moment,' said Granny. 'It's worth a try. So how do we get in?'

'We can't just walk in through the main doors,' said Jamie. 'Is there another way?'

'There's a big shelf about thirty feet up,' said Thorclan.

'Ye-es . . . ,'said Jamie. 'A pity you're not 29 feet 6 inches taller.'

'Correct, sir, but many moons ago, one of our leading scouts, while he was briefly lost . . .'

'Yenech?' asked Granny.

'The same. Yenech found himself inside some narrow flues and passages in that sector, with a door slightly open ahead of him. Through the crack, he saw that it led to the high shelf running round the inside of the Saloon. That still might be a way in.'

After brief discussion, they adopted this, their only, plan. The Marble Saloon it was – via an old passage and onto the shelf. Once inside the room, they might discover more, and up there they'd also be out of human sight.

'The only problem is whether we can get through that door,' said Jamie, pondering the practicalities. 'And if Yenech can remember how he got there.'

'We'll cross that bridge when we come to it,' said Granny.

'There isn't a bridge,' offered Thorclan. 'No, he definitely said nothing about a bridge. If we cross a bridge, we've gone the wrong way.'

'Are you going as well, General?' asked Granny. 'Shouldn't we just use TQS?'

'There's no way that Thorclan, GLOB, SCAB, is going to miss this little job,' he replied, puffing out his chest. 'We might need you big ones down on the ground, but this is a job for the professionals. I'm really going to give my mind to this one.'

'Oh good,' said Jamie, hoping he sounded enthusiastic.

A nervous Nigriff was seated outside the Academic Boardroom in the basement of the Temple of Ancient Virtue. From inside came the chink of glasses and bursts of laughter, until the doors suddenly swung open with a gust of warm air to reveal the beaming and ruddy face of his good friend, Professor Malowit. He had occupied the Chair of Philosophy with great distinction for many years.

'Nigriff, my dear fellow, do come in.' He was shown to a seat in the middle of the room, facing four Board members behind a long table. Professor Malowit took his place in their centre. 'You do know these good people, but allow me to introduce them – and may we address you as "Mr Nigriff"?'

Mr Nigriff nodded.

'Splendid. On my far right is Dr Yungen, Senior Lecturer in

Psychology, currently investigating whether insanity is hereditary – although we do know that you can catch it from your children!' The others laughed warmly. 'Next is Professor Vangor, Head of Mathematics, author of several books with far more numbers than words.' Again, polite laughter. Nigriff managed a faint smile. 'To my far left is Dame Zira Nozna, noted historian, *never* out of date, and finally Dr Twilmid, Reader in Anthropology, Sociology . . . and any other words ending in ology!' The smooth manner of the Chairman put everyone at ease – apart from Nigriff.

The chairman continued. 'Mr Nigriff, after the recent turbulence, happily now over, I was personally asked by the Listener to gather a distinguished panel to consider your ideas. I think a *brief* statement of your thesis would be a good start.'

Nigriff spoke up. 'Honoured members. I am deeply indebted to you for this meeting and also for your continued intellectual leadership.' There were grunts of approval. He paused. 'My thesis is *The Origin of Our Species*. It suggests that our people once lived on an island kingdom. An island called Lilliput.'

The reaction wasn't *too* hostile. Professor Malowit sighed and Dame Nozna uttered, 'Myths, just myths.' Professor Vangor looked cross and Twilmid shook his head slowly, murmuring, 'Poor fellow.' Dr Yungen raised a hand. 'I'd like to ask a simple but very *personal* question. Mr Nigriff, did you have a miserable *childhood*?'

Nigriff was shocked. 'No, Dr Yungen. My parents loved me, I had notable success at school . . . .'

'But not at sports . . . other children resented your intellect . . . and your only friends were old documents. Mr Nigriff, are you trying to compensate for your inadequate background by inventing a *perfect* world in the past?'

Nigriff was lost for words, although 'rubbish' came to mind.

Dame Nozna, the historian, spoke up. 'Mr Nigriff, despite the perceptive theory of my learned colleague, we need some hard *evidence*. Do any documents in the Archives support your claim?'

'Indeed, Madam. An early map shows Lilliput's regions matching exactly our four provinces. For example, Elysium is where the library and schools were.'

Twilmid snorted. 'You're not *seriously* suggesting that this mythical island decided our own settlement patterns?'

'I am not *suggesting*, sir. I'm stating the historical evidence.'

Dame Nozna smiled sympathetically. 'An intelligent man like yourself *must* realise that the mapmakers might have just imitated *our* patterns. Chickens and eggs, Mr Nigriff. Or should I say, 'don't count your chickens?'

'I say, how clever!' exclaimed Twilmid, enjoying the witticism.

'So where is this island?' butted in Professor Vangor. 'Can we go there?'

Nigriff knew this was a weakness. 'I'm afraid not, Professor. It is, er . . . hard to locate at present.' Silence.

'And how did we get to here from this 'hard-to-locate' island? Swim?'

'We were kidnapped, Professor.'

'By a human presumably?'

'Yes, his name was Biddle. He was a sea-captain.'

Professor Malowit interrupted. 'The fiendish name that superstitious parents threaten their children with? Are you saying he actually existed?'

'Yes, Professor.'

'But presumably no more?' said Vangor mockingly. 'Hard to locate perhaps?'

'Of course, Professor; he no longer exists.' The panel exchanged jokey comments. Nigriff continued. 'But his descendant does. He planned the kidnap of Yenech and the others.' Their laughter ceased.

Professor Malowit took charge. 'Mr Nigriff, let's be serious. You are honestly claiming that we are at the mercy of the distant relation of a diabolical fantasy figure, who once rampaged round a fictional island?' He paused. 'It won't do, I'm afraid.'

'Your *lost* childhood,' said Dr Yungen, 'may have led to a belief in . . .'

'Mr Nigriff,' interrupted Dame Nozna, 'when our unfortunate ancestors arrived at Malplaquet, where did they live?'

He appreciated a serious question. 'On an island on the Eleven-Acre Lake.'

'*Another* island?' snapped Vangor. 'Oh, good. Can we visit *that* one?'

'No, unfortunately, it has also . . . disappeared.'

'Like your theory,' replied the fuming Professor of Mathematics. 'Do you know the chances of two islands just *vanishing*? Precisely *nil*.'

Dame Nozna was pursuing the history. 'After the second island - what then?'

'The Lilliputians lived in a model village in the Japanese Gardens.'

'Which – surprise, surprise – isn't *there* any more!' exclaimed Vangor. 'Do you know what's going to disappear next? Yours truly! Children might believe this fantasy, but nobody with half a brain. Like me!' He stormed out, slamming the door.

After a brief silence, Professor Malowit gathered his thoughts. 'Nigriff, we go back a long way, but I have to say your evidence is not compelling . . . or even *existing*. Has anything else convinced you of the truth of your beliefs? And please, nothing else that has disappeared.'

Nigriff knew this was his last chance. 'There is *much* more. In my safekeeping is an ancient poem by Alexander Pope, predicting the appearance of a great Guide who will create a mighty Empire, and Jamie Thompson fits these prophecies. Our Empire *is* growing stronger. There have also been *unusual* recent occurrences.' He paused for breath. 'Increasingly strong forces are changing us into *one* people. Lilliput *is* starting to reappear.' He stopped, emotionally tired.

'At least *something* is reappearing, and not *vanishing*,' muttered Dame Nozna.

'Exactly *what* toys did your parents give you?' asked Dr Yungen.

Twilmid was musing. 'Myths of perfect islands occur in *many* cultures . . . .'

Professor Malowit got to his feet. He gently walked Nigriff to the door, an arm around his shoulder. Out of the panel's earshot, he spoke quietly to his friend. 'I couldn't say so in there, but you *might* be on to something, old chap, but I *can't* take the risk at the moment; there's my Faculty, never mind my publishers . . . .' They were standing in the corridor. 'Do yourself a favour; don't rush to any conclusions, keep me informed, and get some sleep. Thanks for coming, Nigriff; very stimulating.'

Nigriff shook hands, turned to go, and after a few steps heard Malowit's voice. 'Oh, I forgot – have you used the Archives' new Answering and Selection Service? Isn't it the worst thing ever? I'll break that girl's violin in half one day . . .'

Bleynet was glad that this was his last night of guard-duty in the Grecian Valley. The first part of the week hadn't been too bad; a bunch of hyper-active young rabbits had shown him round a 'totally awesome' new warren they'd dug, and a group of hedgehogs had spent a couple of hours one night with him reminiscing about 'the good old days.'

But tonight was different; not only had he forgotten his penny-whistle, which often helped to alleviate the boredom, but there was also a full moon, which was casting odd shadows as it danced in and out of clouds. For example, as he looked up towards the pediment of their Grecian Temple, it was almost possible to believe that the turtle was slowly walking along the front ledge. Indeed, Bleynet now realised to his horror, it *was* doing exactly that, gently dragging itself along, head swaying from side to side. And the hawk, seated on the hand of a tunic-clad boy, was extending its wings and stretching its neck, staring into the distance in search of prey.

'Guard-duty is not meant to be like this,' Bleynet said to himself. Nervously he got up from the grass and began to walk back through the woods.

It was the scurrying in the bushes that really made him jump, a quick rustling of leaves as if being brushed aside. Fortunately for him, Bleynet didn't actually see the lizard-like creature, which was at least five times his size – nor indeed the monkey, scrambling up a nearby tree. These noises were not the usual sounds of the night; Bleynet broke into a run, looking around anxiously, and trying to remember where the nearest badger sets were. The thudding of a horse's hooves on the open grass made his heart beat even faster, and he began to think about the other animals from the pediment – such as the camel, or the alligator . . . .

He ran on, panting rapidly. And then at last he saw it. Picked out in the moonlight not far ahead, he spotted a rounded hole at the foot of a tree, and sped furiously onwards, only stopping by the trunk to get his breath back, not wanting to rush in uninvited.

That was a big mistake of course. The warm and moist air blown around his neck from behind was, in some ways, a relief from the chill of the night, but it was also enough to send him careering down the badger-hole to its furthermost end. Which was a pity, because he missed the truly wonderful sight of the male lion, standing between two lionesses, with its glorious mane catching the moonlight.

Bleynet never did any night-time duties again. Much to his relief and the envy of his mates, he found himself working with the new re-cruits; his stories, so realistically and dramatically told in a darkened room under the Temple, were a helpful test of the trainees' courage and mental strength under pressure. And from then on, any Grecian who claimed they had experienced something similar at night was labelled as 'doing a Bleynet' and understandably disbelieved.

Mr and Mrs Thompson were delighted but confused by Jamie's easy start to Malplaquet School. They were delighted because he had expressed no unhappiness whatsoever; in fact, he had expressed hardly anything. And that was also why they were confused. Even at the end of the first day, when he had returned home and his parents had pumped him for information, everything had been 'cool,' 'okay,' or 'alright.' This had really thrown Mrs Thompson.

Her husband had tried to explain. 'But darling, don't you remember what it's like being thirteen? The last people you want to speak to are your parents.'

'Really?' Mrs Thompson had replied. 'When I was thirteen, I spoke to them non-stop. But if *you* didn't chat to yours much, it's hardly surprising that Jamie . . . .'

To calm their growing anxieties, they had resorted to over-hearing his phone conversations with Granny, who was getting far more of his time than they were. Obviously not *deliberately* over-hearing, because that would have been wrong, so they made sure that it happened purely by accident.

And that gave them a second reason for being confused.

The snippets of information revealed that his best friends sounded like Floorclean and Midriff. 'They can't be their *real* names,' said Mrs Thompson, thumbing through the school list. 'I can't find anybody called that.'

'Nicknames,' said Mr Thompson. 'Bound to be. My best friends at school were Bigbum, Four-eyes, Greasy and Slobber.'

'My best friends were Helena, Judith, Hilary and Rosemary,' replied Mrs Thompson. 'What sort of friends did you have?'

Their only consolation from these moments of fortuitous eavesdropping had occurred recently. Jamie had mentioned, 'gaining the capital,' which had excited his Dad.

'It can only mean one thing,' he whispered to his wife, trying to keep his voice down. 'Money! He's obviously persuaded the old dear not just to spend her investments on school fees, but to cash in a lump sum as well. Smart boy!'

Mrs Thompson wondered if her husband was going slowly mad. She decided it was probably Bigbum's fault. Or maybe Slobber's.

'It's a long time since I've had a good nose around the mansion,' said Granny, 'and of course I've never crawled along those little passages that Yenech found.'

They were poring over their drawing of the mansion's groundplan on a roll of wallpaper, trying to work out a route onto the high shelf in the Marble Saloon. A line of impressive State Rooms ran along the length of the building.

'Starting from the east end, we could go through the Blue Room, into the Library, and then past the Music Room,' said Jamie.

'Far too difficult,' said Granny, scratching her chin. 'The west is much better.'

'Why?' asked Jamie.

'There are lots of old heating flues on that side, from a huge fireplace down below in the basement corridor. It warmed the western rooms through those shafts and some pipes – and the Marble Saloon by a large brass vent in the middle of the floor.'

'Perfect!' exclaimed Thorclan. 'That vent's the way in for the Grecian Army. I can see it already. What we'll do is . . . .'

'Go another way,' said Granny. 'It's been concreted in.'

'Plan B is much safer anyway,' urged Thorclan, not to be outwitted.

'The problem is, those flues probably go everywhere,' said Granny.

'Where do I come into all this?' enquired Yenech, who had stirred on the words 'go everywhere.'

'You and Hyroc and Wesel are the forward party,' said Jamie. 'Thorclan will be following behind with his team.'

'Excellent,' said Yenech enthusiastically. 'I love exploring new places.'

'It's not *new*, Yenech – you've been there before,' said Granny.

'I have?' said Yenech. 'Are you sure?'

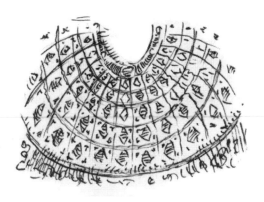

5 : Gaining the Capital

Even after only a few days of term, the gardens surrounding Malplaquet School were already becoming a welcoming retreat for John Biddle. The Manor in Chackmore was so full of builders and wreckers, so full of noise and dust, that the peace and quiet amongst the temples and lake-side walks was immensely calming and refreshing. Not that he found any more company there than at the Manor, for Malplaquet was often deserted, with not another soul to be seen across its grassy acres. However, it never *felt* empty, and neither did John whilst he was there.

He always had a definite sense of being somewhere full of life.

This feeling might easily have been explained by the huge amount of wildlife hiding amongst the bushes and shrubs. It was hard to actually set eyes on any of the smaller mammals and rodents, apart from the ubiquitous squirrels of course, but John could tell from the regular and frantic scurryings under the leaves that Malplaquet was a veritable haven for tiny animals. He sometimes tried to surprise them by tiptoeing nearer and nearer, and once or twice he thought he got pretty close, but they always managed to make good their escape just before he pulled back the branches.

This lunchtime, however, his timing was almost absolutely perfect. Hearing quiet nibblings somewhere behind a viburnum, he dashed forward, and a pile of dusty leaves swirled up as the creatures scuttled away. John assumed they were probably mice, or maybe young rabbits, but whatever they were, he was surprised to find some dolls' items on the grass nearby – two tiny plates, cups and a shoe. Thinking they were worthless toys left by a careless child, he picked them up and was about to drop them in a nearby bin, when he noticed that they were beautifully made. Placing them instead in his pocket, John wandered off.

'How did he get *so* close?' declared a panting and angry Hoowej, hiding way back in the shadows, annoyed that a pleasant picnic with his new friend had been so rudely interrupted. 'He'd better not have taken our stuff.'

'I knew it was too quiet,' said the young girl, Wigonod. 'That's one of my favourite shoes as well.'

'My Mum won't like it if her dishes disappear,' said Hoowej. 'They're classic Cascadian Hedgewood. I don't know what I'd tell her. If I say we nearly got captured, she'll really have a go at me.' They waited deep in the undergrowth until the coast was clear, and then crept back, only to have their fears confirmed. Their possessions had gone.

'How about saying we tried to fight off a desperate and confused jackdaw,' suggested Hoowej, 'but in the end he nicked some of our things? Would that work?'

'Only if you turn up exhausted,' pondered Wigonod. 'And as I've only got one shoe, you *could* carry me back to the Grecian Temple . . . and then I *might* believe what you say about your Cascadian strength and stamina . . .'

Hoowej smiled. Her plan had a lot to recommend it.

The combined assault on the mansion was planned for the afternoon of the second Saturday of September, when the House would be packed full of visitors for the annual free Heritage Open Day. Jamie and Granny had decided that, with so many people tramping about the place, any sounds of little feet scrambling around would be well and truly hidden. 'Diversionary tactics,' Thorclan had stated, 'to distract their attention. My men know all about that.' As yet, nobody was sure exactly what they were going to do when – or *if* – they found themselves inside the Marble Saloon, but the first problem was to get there. They were hoping the answer lay somewhere within the innermost sanctum.

Further investigation by Jamie had unfortunately revealed that not only had the heating vent in the Saloon's floor been cemented in, but the fireplace below had also been completely blocked a few years ago. There was absolutely no chance of getting inside the old flues that way. Fortunately, however, the most ancient teacher at the school, in reply to a very casual and unusual question from a new boy called Thompson, had confirmed that in previous centuries an enormously long heating pipe had supplied warm air from the mansion's centre to the Orangery at the far western end, as well as to other rooms *en route*. The plotters desperately hoped it still remained open along its entire length – and also connected to the Marble Saloon.

'So, Captain Yassek, can you help us with this route?' Thorclan was quizzing his officer and looking up at the climbing *japonica circumtuitous horizontalis et verticalis,* winding its twisted way up the crumbling wall of the old Orangery.

'It's not a *root*, General; it's the main trunk. I can also inform you, sir, that by a stroke of good fortune, my thesis at Stonehurst Military Academy was "Corridors of Power". Malplaquet's passages featured in a number of my . . . er . . . passages.'

'So what can you tell us abut this magnificent room?'

'It's the *Orangery*, General. Although technically it isn't, because the first Duke used it for the growing of bananas. He wanted to call it the "Bananery", but the Central European lexicographer, Vassop, who grammatically corrected the inscriptions on many monuments during a three-day visit to Malplaquet in 1721, insisted that the proper spelling was Banan*ary* – with an 'a.' The issue was settled by duel with the Duke, in which Vassop ruptured his colon, bringing matters to a full stop. It has remained the Orangery as a sign of disrespect ever since.'

'Capital, Yassek, good to have you on board. Make sure I know other crucial bits of information.' He turned to the troop of men behind him. 'Right, my valiant lads, onwards and upwards! This plant's a climber – if a plant can, we can!' Within a few seconds the tangled mass of leaves and branches was rustling with the sounds of gasping and panting military adventurers.

At the top, they clambered over the ledge of the wall onto the flat roof and brushed bits of leaves and bark off their combats. '*That's* our entrance, gentlemen,' announced Thorclan, pointing towards a rusty vertical tube projecting like a funnel. 'Yenech and the forward party must have gone that way.'

It was a good choice. A small drop down, and they were inside a horizontal metal pipe, with just enough head-height for them. Despite being old it was firm and dry and, as they pushed deeper and deeper into the long building, side-vents gave views of other rooms below. Yassek was a mine of information (he had once worked in Explosives).

'This used to be the *Common* Masters' Room; it was for lesser teachers who didn't have the right sort of degrees or gaiters. And this is the Peasantry, General, where the second Duke kindly allowed the peasants, who had got wet working in his fields, to dry out by hanging over the fires.'

'Are we there yet?' said a voice at the back. 'I'm feeling sick.'

'Stiff upper lip!' shouted Thorclan. 'That should stop it.'

Yassek was in his element. 'And this room, sir, is the Spotted Games Room, where the third Duke, in one of his final bouts of insanity, spent a whole night playing dominoes against his bloodhound. Thinking it had a *paw* hand, he wagered half of Malplaquet Ridings and lost the lot when the dog raised the stakes.'

'Damned clever those bloodhounds,' muttered Thorclan. 'Where are we now?'

'As far as we can go, General. That's a wall.'

'You'll go far, Yassek. Well done.'

Thorclan chose a tunnel on his left, which immediately headed uphill at a rather steep angle. Higher and higher they pressed on, which was a good sign, but there was still no trace of Yenech and his team. That surprised nobody. Hopefully TQS had already made rapid progress.

Indeed they had. Their arduous training programme had massively improved their physical stamina, so they hardly noticed the extra weight of the thread and safety-pins (their specialised climbing equipment). It had also strengthened their team spirit, so they had swarmed along the old flue as one body, encouraging each other to keep moving onwards and upwards at speed. They had eventually found themselves in a length of squared tunnel on the level, and

Yenech, convinced that they now must be on the same floor as the Marble Saloon's cornice, asked Hyroc to poke his head through the next grating to check out the room.

'It's someone's sitting room, seems quiet though. Hang on a minute; I'll get a better look.' He squeezed his face between the bars and peered to his right.

That was why he didn't see the dog watching him on his left.

Nippy the long-haired terrier had been dozing very happily until he had smelt something that *slightly* reminded him of humans – similar, but without the same intensity and strength. Nevertheless, it was *definitely* human, with a whiff of the exotic and unusual, and that made it worth investigating. He managed to give the small creature a quick exploratory lick before it disappeared, but he saw which way it had gone. The tiny human variation also emitted an interesting noise, high-pitched and well beyond a usual person's range, which made it an even more exciting proposition. Playtime!

'It's trying to break in!' screamed Hyroc. 'Run!' But it was too late – the others were already running further and further into the gloom, not knowing what lay ahead of them.

Yenech was the one who fortunately spotted the on-rushing problem just in time – a sudden dark chasm, probably an old chimney flue, extending across the full width of the passage. He slid to a desperate halt, knocking a nail over the edge, which tumbled for ages before pinging unseen on the ground below. Only a few metres back, the dog was scrabbling away at the grille, clouds of dust billowing in, and the occasional bark making them jump and put their hands over their ears.

'Which way now?' yelled Wesel, looking around.

'There's only one way,' replied Yenech. 'Forwards! Use that ledge!'

His instruction was sensible. On the left of the shaft, at floor level, he'd spotted a narrow projection, no wider than their bodies and laden with soot and dust, which traversed the length of the abyss. 'Ropes and pins – now!' Yenech swiftly jammed the first safety-pin into a crack on the wall, passed the thread through and knotted it tight. Giving it a firm pull, he grinned at his mates. 'This is the real thing, gentlemen. One to tell your children about.'

He inched his way forwards, his fingers searching for any slight crevice, his feet kicking away the muck and dust of centuries. Wesel and Hyroc were quietly panicking about the sound of scratching behind them, and the splintering and creaking of wood that was becoming ever more frequent.

Jamie and Vicky, the ground forces, were with a group of tourists being taken round the House by an elderly gentleman in corduroy trousers and a venerable tweed jacket.

'Ladies and Gentlemen, thank you for coming to Malplaquet House, reputed to be one of the finest neo-classical buildings in the whole world. Over the next hour I hope to bring the building to life, and show you things that appear in *few* guidebooks. Our current location, the North Hall, is the least changed room at Malplaquet . . .'

'*I'd* like to see a few things that aren't in the guidebooks,' whispered Jamie. 'I wonder how they're getting on.'

'They might be getting close,' answered Vicky. 'Hey, listen. Is that a dog barking?'

Jamie nodded slowly. 'Are you thinking what I'm thinking?'

'I'm afraid so,' replied Vicky. 'Let's hope it's not lunchtime.'

Yenech edged his way across the final few centimetres, pushed in yet another safety-pin, and tied the last knot. Not far behind, Wesel was making good but nervous progress, holding firmly on to the rope handrail. Hyroc was having greater difficulty. Not convinced the pins were secure, he was fearfully looking down and had consequently slipped a couple of times.

When he was almost halfway across, the heating grille finally yielded to the frantic efforts of the dog, twisted back on itself, cracked, and came away from the wall. Light briefly flooded that end of the tunnel before it was again plunged into gloom by a furry head squeezing into the gap.

'If we've got any luck it won't get through,' said Hyroc, anxiously watching its struggles.

'If we did have any luck, it just ran out,' panted Wesel, watching a terrier pulling its hindquarters through the narrow hole, 'and that's what we should do.'

'I've met a few dogs,' said Yenech, surprisingly confident. 'Trust me; this canyon is far too big for a dog that size to get across.'

The terrier came padding up, and leant over the edge to try to sniff Hyroc, who was encouraged by the hot breath and large tongue to move rather faster. As Yenech had predicted, Nippy decided that the gap was a leap too far merely to gain some sub-human quarry.

He would have to be really scared to make that sort of jump.

Thorclan and his men had also heard the barking and fearing the same as Jamie and Vicky, had jogged along more rapidly. Yassek provided more useful information *en route*. 'General, we are now approaching the Tapestry Room, forever linked with Lady Katherine, the sister of the first Marchioness. She spent many a happy day seated here creating the most wonderful designs, until one day she accidentally sewed herself into her own picture. The lady was looked after for many months on the lower landing of the Kent staircase, and was greatly admired by George III on his state visit.'

At that poignant moment they spotted their foe, Thorclan signalling to his men to come to a halt. Three metres in front sat a sooty terrier, bemused but curious. Nippy quickly decided that, although he had lost his first quarry, he was happy to check out the new supplies. He inched forward, nose sniffing the ground.

'When you see the whites of its eyes,' whispered Thorclan.

'They're brown, General,' said Cherbut.

'In that case – charge!' shouted Thorclan. Nippy wasn't prepared for this phalanx of screaming tiny creatures, waving sticks and blocking its escape. The dog was not a brave terrier; years of chasing aged rabbits had tamed his wilder instincts. He had only one option, and took it magnificently. Timing the approach to perfection, he soared across the dark gap and landed safely on the other side.

'That showed it who's boss,' declared Thorclan. 'Pity Yenech missed this.' He then spotted the rope handrail on the left of the hole, looked at his officers who were clearly thinking the same thing, and made a quick decision. 'Forward!' shouted the leader. 'Terror to the terrier!'

Vicky and Jamie were deliberately obstructing the doors leading from the North Hall into the Marble Saloon. They could cause a distraction if needed – and after a loud thump up on the high shelf, followed by a faint pattering noise, it clearly *was* needed.

'Excuse me, sir,' said Jamie politely, as Vicky held the Saloon doors behind them, 'but you said the picture on the ceiling was Mars giving a sword away. Why is he painted like an old soldier – and not a planet – nor even a bar of chocolate?' This was followed by further unusual questions that the guide had never been asked, which used up some precious minutes.

Elsewhere Yenech, Wesel and Hyroc had been relieved that the passage ended in a door that was easy to push open. They were even more delighted that it actually did lead out onto the Saloon's high shelf, circling the domed ceiling that rose up to a large central window (technically called an *oculus*). Just above that shelf, parading around the entire room, was a sculptured frieze of a Roman Army in a victory procession.

TQS were not pleased, however, that they were still being chased by a dog, which had somehow found the determination (or the fear) to leap the void.

The dog wasn't pleased that it was still being chased by some mad and unfamiliar miniature creatures.

'Round the far side, quick!' shouted Yenech, 'and climb up by that person on the chariot!'

Nippy was gingerly padding his way along the side facing the North Hall entrance. He had not gone very far when Thorclan's army arrived. The General was sorely tempted to stop and gaze at the awe-inspiring stone display of military muscle, but he knew he had to assess the situation very quickly. 'Right, chaps, the old pincer movement should achieve our goal – the forwards can work the flanks, supported by fast overlapping defenders. Anybody want to plug the gap in midfield?'

The tactics worked brilliantly. The soldiers on the left wing whipped round to the far end, swept past the chariot with its new occupants, and prevented Nippy from moving any further along the cornice. A simultaneous attack down the right wing meant that the terrier was hemmed in by tiny people sneaking along, hissing and jabbing with their tiny spears. He might never live this down; if the rabbits ever found out, they'd be laughing for weeks. He sat there, trapped, miserable and defeated.

Jamie and Vicky could detain the tour guide no longer, as he was becoming increasingly irritated by Jamie's observations. 'No, Alexander the Great is not engaged in a bout of arm-wrestling with her . . . ! We now simply *must* enter the Marble Saloon, one of our most spectacular rooms.' He paused for dramatic effect. 'Your eyes will be drawn not just to the noble dome, but also to the frieze below it. In fact, here's a question for the children.' He was pleased at his ability to engage an audience of all ages. 'When I open the doors, if you look up, you'll see an animal about to be sacrificed by a priest. Who can tell me what it is?'

With a great flourish, he threw the doors open behind him and was delighted to observe the reaction of the crowd. Absolute silence; mouth wide-open silence. Never before had he seen a group so dumb-struck by their first sight of the Marble Saloon and its sculptures. He was surprised, however, that the children were taking so long to identify the carved bull by the altar.

'Come, come,' he urged. 'You must have seen one before. It's about to have a knife plunged into it. Can anyone tell me before it dies? Anybody?' A little girl began to sob and pull back towards the doors. 'Any adults then?'

Her father spoke up. 'It's a dog, mister, any fool can see that – and he doesn't look happy. You're sick – you should be reported.'

The bewildered guide managed to retrieve the situation. He sent an assistant to find a workman with a long ladder, explained away his unfortunate comments, and only five of his party left the room. Jamie and Vicky were pleased that only the *dog* had been noticed, although they themselves had spotted three new riders on the chariot.

The guide continued with his commentary. 'To my right, ladies and gentlemen – and I'm having a *very* careful look first – is the female figure of Victory in the *biga* or two-horse chariot.' Jamie surreptitiously motioned to the three figures to stay hidden. 'She is riding in style, the focus of the adulation of the Roman people, the victorious General walking below her. Soon he will clamber up onto the very chariot itself, a position which shows that he has received the Freedom of the City of Rome. Or, to use the more correct phrase, he will have *gained the capital*.'

Jamie and Vicky looked at each other in astonishment and then at the three heroes. Three heroes who had gained the capital. But the guide's final words were followed by the most enormous flash of light and a loud crash, clattering the oval oculus high above them, and causing everybody to rush out onto the South Front. A thunderbolt had flashed down right into the middle of the cricket pitch, leaving a small hole with jagged burn marks searing away from it.

The only people left inside were Jamie and Vicky (jumping up and down, slapping their palms in high-fives), a collection of soldiers standing below a stone chariot and cheering like mad, and three people above them waving in reply. A small terrier also spotted a sudden gap in the defence and disappeared through a small door, determined never again to chase anything that smelt remotely human.

The capital had undoubtedly been gained, easily and quickly, and Jamie was absolutely thrilled. Victory was theirs!

However, there was one thing that puzzled him. Just as the searing light had flashed around the vast room, he had noticed something, a split-second of rapid activity high up amongst the sculptures. One of the horses pulling the chariot had swiftly reared up, its front legs pawing the air. By the time that Jamie had blinked and looked up again at the carving, it was all over, and the triumphant figures were stuck in their usual stony poses.

Jamie tried not to think about it too much for the moment; it had to be a trick of the light. Anyway, Vicky was grabbing him by the arm and they were running outside.

6 : New Faces

'That *dear* little dog,' said Granny, looking across the table at Jamie, 'must have been scared out of its wits. Those poor children as well – thinking it was going to be sacrificed!'

'They definitely weren't happy,' said Jamie. 'A pity you missed it all, Nigriff – you'd have been really proud of your team-mates in that chariot.'

'I *am* proud of them, Master Jamie,' replied Nigriff, 'proud beyond words. I also regret my failure to play an active part in the campaign.'

'Nigriff, *you* were doing what you could,' reassured Granny. 'Nobody else could have taken on the collected brains of the Academic Board like you did.'

'I appreciate your over-generous praise,' answered Nigriff, 'but if you are wondering what word best describes my efforts with them, you will find that "*feeble*" fits perfectly.'

'Don't worry about it, Nigriff,' said Jamie, 'at least another piece of the jigsaw – or the prophecy – is in place. We *have* gained the capital.'

'That phrase,' said Granny, 'has been bothering me. It could mean all sorts of things – like getting some money, for example – but I suppose you're right.'

'*Definitely*,' stated Jamie firmly. 'The noise of the thunderbolt was awesome, and a Science teacher ran straight to where it hit, and his gown billowed up with all the static. Wicked.'

Discussion returned to Pope's poem. Were any of its verses yet to be fulfilled? The old box was brought out and the ancient paper gently flattened on the table. They all again read the extraordinary prophecy about the great leader and the new Empire.

'I can't see anything else,' offered Granny after a while. 'You passed those Three Tests right at the start, Jamie, and the people *are* becoming more united. All four "*quarters*" – the provinces – are being defended and now we've "*gained the capital*". That seems to be about it.'

'How about "*borders sealed*"?' asked Jamie.

'That, sir, must refer to the noble efforts of the stout General . . . sorry, the stout efforts of the noble General. I do apologise, my mind's rather muddled.'

'What you're saying, Nigriff,' suggested Granny, 'is that the Grecians have secured the frontiers – correct?'

'Thank you, Madam, that is indeed my interpretation of that line.'

Jamie was still looking at the poem. 'Interesting that it mentions "*this blessed island*",' said Jamie thoughtfully. 'Obviously at the time Pope meant Britain, but now that we know that Malplaquet is shaped like Lilliput, maybe it means this place as well.'

They all considered this interesting idea, and had to agree that, yes, it could mean that the Guide would one day help the little people to live in a place that resembled an island. *Their* island.

'Hmm,' murmured Nigriff. 'That is an appealing concept; the citizens of Lilliput living on an isolated country estate, which has a similar outline to their old homeland. It cannot be the same as the *real* thing, of course, but perhaps . . . perhaps it is the best one can hope for. . . .' He became quiet, lost in his thoughts, a far-away look in his eye.

Jamie and Granny looked at the little Archivist, whose ancestors had once freely and happily walked the hills of Lilliput, lived in its dwellings, worked the fields and breathed its air. Wistful thoughts – even *emotions* – were stirring deep within the poor chap.

'I'm really sorry, Nigriff,' said Granny gently, holding out an open hand towards him. 'I didn't realise Lilliput meant so much to you.'

'Esteemed lady,' replied Nigriff, 'neither did I, neither did I. I am not sure what has provoked it.' He paused and swallowed. 'I have always known about the Empire, its history, the great sagas of Lilliput, but until this moment it has been mere *words* – names and dates in documents, events to be noted and facts to be checked.'

'And now it's starting to mean a lot more,' said Granny.

Nigriff nodded. 'It's almost as if . . . almost . . ,' and again he paused, struggling to express himself. 'As if . . . I *miss* it. I've never been there; there's no evidence that it still exists, yet it seems *close by* . . . How can that be?' His voice was trembling.

After a brief silence amongst the three, Granny made a thoughtful suggestion. 'Nigriff, maybe it's because these gardens remind you of Lilliput. I'm sure it's their shape, like Jamie has said.' Her words were kindly meant but did nothing to lighten the little man's sadness.

Jamie spoke up. 'But it's not just the *shape*s. That old map showed that the four provinces exactly match the island's regions. It's strange.'

'*Far* too strange,' said Granny. 'We'll never be able to work that out.'

'We *have* to,' urged Jamie, 'it *has* to make sense.' He looked at them. 'Let's think about it. We know the *restored* temples are affecting humans, making them appreciate the place and see all sorts of things. Right?'

They nodded in agreement. Jamie slowly spelt out his conclusion.

'But those temples affect the *Lilliputians* as well – like in Elysium, *precisely* where the schools were in Lilliput, Ancient Virtue made Thorclan clever. It's like some power is coming through them. As if Lilliput *is* still around.'

Nigriff looked lost for words, but did his best. 'A remarkable idea, Master Jamie.' He paused. 'I have always *believed* in Lilliput,' he said carefully, 'but as only an idea in my *mind*. Now . . . now I fear I can *feel* it.' He sighed; the longing expressed in his words was very moving.

Suddenly he pulled himself together. 'I am becoming far too emotional,' he declared. 'Clearly a self-pitying reaction to my deserved defeat by the assorted academics. I *must* return at once to my books and my research.'

Jamie, although relieved that the *logical* Nigriff was still around, was unsure about his final comment. 'What research, Nigriff?'

'My investigation into the Alcove,' replied Nigriff. 'It is still required of me.' After a signal to Granny, who lowered him gently to the floor, he scurried out.

'It's beginning to get to him,' said Jamie. Granny nodded her agreement.

Sunday tea-time and Jamie was being given the Third Degree treatment by his parents about his first few days at Malplaquet School.

'Lunches alright, are they?' asked Dad.

'Er, yeh, they're fine,' said Jamie.

'You see, the trouble is, Jamie,' said Mum, 'that we've hardly seen you this week. You hang around down at Granny's straight after school each day – and don't get me wrong, I don't mind, she is paying the fees after all – but when you come home, you just bolt down your food, fly upstairs and just stay in your room.'

'Er, sorry,' said Jamie, not sure if that was what he was meant to say.

'And then when I do check to see if you're doing your work, you're still reading about gardens and Alexander Pope. That can't be homework, surely?'

'It's Vis Ed,' replied Jamie. 'My favourite subject.'

'Nothing wrong with that,' said Dad, 'and at least we've now found out *one* thing. Anything more you can tell us?'

'What else do you want to know?'

'Any friends you've made this week?' said Mum.

'Exactly!' said Dad. 'Tell us about two of your friends, Floorclean and Midriff.'

Charlie burst out laughing, which was just as well because it diverted attention away from Jamie, whose mind was racing. It sounded as if his father had mispronounced Thorclan and Nigriff.

'Sorry,' said Jamie, 'what did you say?'

'*Floorclean* and *Midriff*,' said Dad carefully, deliberately emphasizing every syllable and consonant. He held up a threatening hand to Charlie, who was having trouble holding his breath. 'I just happened to overhear you on the phone. That's obviously not their *proper* names, but nicknames, right?

'Ye-es,' said Jamie, with some hesitation and also relief. 'Nicknames, sure.'

'Fine,' said Mum. 'So what are these two like?'

'They're smaller than me,' replied Jamie, thinking fast. 'One's really smart and uses lots of long words, and the other is into soldiers and armies. He's not as clever as the other one.'

'So which is which?' asked Mum.

Jamie thought it best to confuse the picture. 'Umm . . . Floorclean's the clever one. . . .'

'Which is why he's Floorclean,' interrupted Dad knowingly. 'Bright and sparkling, wipes the floor with everybody in tests.' He congratulated himself on his grasp of adolescent male logic. 'Presumably Midriff is tubby around the waist?'

'Er, yes,' replied Jamie.

'And their real names are?' asked Mum, thinking this conversation would not be happening with a daughter.

'Dunno,' said the son.

'You don't *know*?' she spluttered in astonishment.

Dad came to Jamie's rescue. 'But that's how it is with boys. It was weeks before I found out the real names of Slobber and Bigbum.'

Charlie couldn't contain himself any longer; he exploded spectacularly in a fit of laughter, and was inevitably sent out of the room. His older brother seized the opportunity to make good his own escape.

'By the way,' whispered Charlie as they made their way upstairs, 'your secret's safe with me for the moment.'

Jamie tried not to show his surprise. 'Secret?' he asked, hoping he sounded relaxed and nonchalant.

'Yep,' said Charlie, very pleased with himself. '*Maria.* I know all about her.'

Jamie stopped on the top stair. 'Like what?'

'Only that she's your girlfriend, and she's got you interested in flowers and poetry – and gave you that book about Malplaquet to read.'

Jamie smiled quietly to himself. 'Fine,' he said, 'but it's not like that. We're just good friends.'

'Yeh, right,' said Charlie, satisfied with his success. 'Just remember, this little bit of information is valuable.' He began to count out imaginary coins into his hands.

'No chance,' grunted Jamie. 'Say what you like – I don't care.'

'Oh, I think you will,' said Charlie smugly. 'I think you will.'

Chackmore Manor had three very poky rooms right at the top of the house, squeezed into the roof-space years ago to contain servants or unwanted furniture. This Sunday evening, a young boy was hunched in one corner on the edge of a mattress, his arms folded tightly around him. John Biddle stared into empty space, not really noticing the dust, the dull mud-brown walls, and the grey small window that showed heavy clouds outside. Nearby were two old trunks, probably containing some of his books and games, but tightly locked. By the mattress was a pile of crumpled clothes, some needing to be washed and others to wear for school next week. Somehow they'd all ended up in the same pile. Outside was the noise of chainsaws, shouts, the reverberation of engines and the intrusive bleeps of reversing vehicles.

John was thinking about his first week at Malplaquet School. Each morning had begun in the same dismal way; he'd creep downstairs into the cavernous basement kitchens and find some bread or a half-empty milk carton amongst the tea-cups swimming with cigarette ends. The first morning he'd been caught by a large woman in stained white overalls; 'Get a move on, kid,' she'd shouted, 'it'll take you half an hour to walk there!' John had hurried out, confused that there was nobody to drive him, but he assumed it was his own fault. He must have forgotten an instruction; his father often had to remind him about his poor memory.

In fact, the long walk had become a time to treasure. In the mornings, as he had trudged up the long slope towards the Corinthian Arch, once or twice getting wet with rain, he had usually been greeted by various dog-walkers. He'd gradually begun to recognise some of them, and this made him feel part of the place, as if he belonged. Then it was past the Arch, with its wonderful views across the fields and lakes towards the mansion, kicking along the woodland track to the Bell Gate, and then the magical moment when he was confronted with the most glorious sight. First the Octagon Lake, then, beyond it, the wide sweep of smooth lawns flowing up the slope, and on its brow the majestic and golden South Front of Malplaquet House, presiding over all.

Each morning this vista had lifted his spirits. And something he vaguely recognised as feelings of delight, even joy, stirred within him.

He'd also noticed a cottage built onto the back of a lakeside pavilion and, late one afternoon on the way back to the Manor he'd bumped into the old lady who lived there.

She had been leaning over her gate, chatting to a group of children filing past on horseback. He'd tried to shuffle along without being noticed, but she had called out, 'Hello there, just started at the school?' John had nodded and mumbled a quick reply, and then had ducked behind the line of horses and carried on. The woman had seemed friendly enough, but he hadn't wanted to get involved in a conversation, or say much about himself, with lots of other children around. He didn't know what they were like or what they might think of him.

These various thoughts, comforting John's present isolation in his bedroom, were suddenly scattered by a single inevitable one – homework! 'See what you can find out about . . ,' the teachers had said. 'Use the internet or ask your parents for help.' His father had bought him a very expensive computer, but it hadn't been dropped off yet, and the second suggestion just wasn't realistic.

So John kept returning to the same reluctant conclusion; he would have to go downstairs to the Study. He wasn't allowed in there by himself. One of his worst memories was his father shouting in his face. It happened on a rainy day when John was about six in the study of a previous house, when John had been looking at the pictures in some big books on the carpet when his father found him. He still did not know what he had done wrong, but he knew it must have been something awful because the feeling about it was horrible.

In spite of this, ten minutes later John was crouching behind the banisters at the top of the stairs, watching and waiting. Soon a man with armfuls of long cardboard tubes approached the study door, punched in four numbers on the keypad, left the items inside and pulled the door after him.

As soon as it was safe, John tiptoed down the stairs, pressed the same code, and he was in.

He was shocked at the state of the room; everywhere else in the house was in chaos but the study was immaculate. The polished mahogany panelling that he recognized from their last place was already fitted, shelves and cupboard doors were numbered and labelled, and rows of books and document boxes were standing ready for inspection. On the walls hung maps and charts, the enormous mahogany desk was set out with pens and small containers, and a game of chess had been started on a small side-table. The windows were all fitted with vertical bars as usual.

John read the labels on the shelves. 'Tax and Investments . . . Exploration . . . Biological Procedures . . . Country Houses of England and Wales.' He scanned the last section, looking for one to help with his Vis Ed homework. He soon found one entitled *The Origins of the English Landscape Garden*. Next to it was one with a deep red cover called *Mistress Masham's Repose*. The title intrigued him. He opened it up, and found a drawing of an estate headed, 'The Palace of Malplaquet.' He thought he recognized some of the buildings in the grounds. Placing these two books on the floor, he moved along to a cupboard with an unnamed pair of doors. He tugged at them, and when they opened he stepped back in shock.

Inside, staring at him, was a pure white face, slightly larger than life size. It was carved, with hard eyes and a firm expression. John let his eyes drop to the incised lettering on the base of the stone bust: 'John Biddle.'

'Get away from that! What are you doing here?' The angry shout from behind made him jump. John turned to see a man pointing a walking-stick at him.

'Sorry, it's for my homework, I need some books.' John bent down and grabbed the two. The man strode over and shut the cupboard doors, turning a key in the lock.

'Out! How did you get in here anyway?'

'The door was open – I was going past.'

'Don't let me *ever* catch you in here again.' His hand tightened on his stick. 'If your father finds out . . .'

John ran up the stairs to his room. He threw himself onto his mattress, only too aware that he had been bad again, but relieved that he had some books – and excited that he had seen a statue of his famous ancestor. He wondered why it was kept locked away; it must be very valuable.

'Is this training *really* necessary?' said Granny to her wicker basket. She was setting up a large umbrella by the side of Copper Bottom Lake, a steady drizzle dampening everything. Yenech's head popped out from the container. 'All part of our routine, Madam – and it's late afternoon, away from tourists, and it's raining. It'll be fine.'

'Fine?' grumbled Thorclan, struggling to get a leg over the edge of the basket. 'The forecast is rain. Lots of it. This is Navy weather, not Army. If I'd wanted to get wet, I'd have become an Admiral, not a General.'

Granny gave Thorclan a hand, then pulled the small rowing boat out of its plastic bag and placed it at the water's edge. Wesel and Hyroc had already grabbed the pair of oars (fashioned from kebab skewers and lollipop sticks) and settled down side by side on the central seat.

'It's the visibility thing that bothers me,' muttered Granny, 'but I suppose the radio will help if somebody does happen to see you.'

'It's a brainwave,' said Yenech. 'Point the aerial over the lake. If anybody does turns up, they'll just think you're controlling the boat. TQS? OK?'

Wesel and Hyroc slapped their right arms on their chest and said in unison, 'TQS – your problem is *us*!'

'Well, if you're sure,' said Granny, helping Thorclan to step across into the bow. He sat down heavily, rocking the boat, facing Yenech who was holding the tiller. He cleared his throat, nodded to Granny who gave the boat a gentle push away from the bank, and gave his first nautical command.

'By the left, quick, pull!'

The craft moved round in a perfect circle. Granny was fiddling with the knobs on the radio, already rather worried.

'Halt!' ordered the new Commander. 'As you were.' The two oarsmen stopped rowing and the boat slowly glided to a stop. 'Let's try again . . . must be a new set of orders . . . Ready? Pull – left, right, left, right.'

The boat swerved from side to side across the lake, Yenech trying to correct the swinging motion with the tiller but only making it worse. They were all, including Granny, concentrating so hard on the boat's erratic progress that nobody noticed the flat-bed truck driving down the hill towards the Temple of Venus.

The volunteers, holding on tight on the back, had fencing materials for a job next week – heavy stakes, wire and rolls of netting.

'Now I've seen everything – an old lady playing with her radio-controlled boat in the rain,' said one of the men.

'Her first time, judging by the mess she's making of it,' said another.

'Smart boat though,' said a third quietly. 'Even got models in it.'

'I think I know her,' said Vicky. She stood up as the truck slowed. 'Yoo-hoo,' she shouted, waving her arms frantically.

The old lady was surprised, but waved back.

'Watch the controls, my dear!' came a man's shout. 'Nearly lost the boat.' It had suddenly executed a steep turn, causing the model figure in the bow to fall back off its seat and onto its rear end with a thump, its legs sticking up in the air.

'Don't move, General,' muttered Yenech through tight lips. 'We're being watched. Right chaps, automatic pilot now . . . together, pull . . . like robots . . . pull.'

'I think she's got the hang of it now,' said Vicky. 'C'mon, let's go.'

'Not me,' insisted Ralph quickly, 'I want a closer look.' He jumped off the back of the truck and was away, slipping and sliding down the slope to the lake.

Vicky reacted quickly. 'Me too,' she said and leapt off after him.

Granny saw what was happening and began to panic, pushing all the buttons she could find, causing a deep and cultured voice to crackle over the water; *'Dogger and German Bight, westerly, gale force six.'* Thorclan was getting facefuls of water from the steady splashing above him, and Yenech was sat as still as a statue.

Ralph didn't know what hit him, but it was Vicky, slithering in from behind and shouting, 'Oops, sorry!' and knocking him into the cold lake. It was shallow enough for him to immediately kneel up and catch hold of her outstretched hand.

The boat, caught by the small tidal waves from his ungainly dive, was swept across to the opposite bank. Thorclan's legs were still stuck up like a small pair of masts. His final indignity was to be lifted out upside-down by his feet by Granny, who pretended to straighten out his limbs. She watched Vicky leading the soggy Ralph back to the lorry.

'That,' she said, 'was lucky.'

'That,' said Yenech, 'was fantastic. Well done, TQS! And bravo to the new Admiral – or should we call you *Rear* Admiral, sir?'

'Not funny, soldier,' groaned Thorclan, tenderly rubbing his posterior. 'I think I've worked out why this lake is called Copper Bottom . . . and it's not nice.'

7 : Uncovering The Past

Mr. Merryman, who taught Visual Education, was noted for his bouncy enthusiasm and never-failing good humour. Facing his new class on the grassy North Front, he was joyfully explaining how Malplaquet House behind him had changed over the last three hundred years. The boys were only just hanging on to photocopied handouts that were flapping in the stiff breeze.

'We can see a lot more when we're outside the classroom,' he said cheerily. A gust of wind swept a mass of his greying wavy hair across his face and he struggled to keep it out of his eyes. A boy at the back sniggered. 'Thank you, Stafford, I *can* still see you,' advised Merryman. 'Right, a little test. Question number one – what's in *front* of you?'

A small boy directly below him, so close as to be almost touching his waistcoat, fired his hand in the air and a jabbing finger nearly entered Merryman's left nostril. The teacher took a step back to protect his facial features.

'Yes, Johnstone?'

'You, sir.'

'Indeed, Johnstone, but I meant *behind* me. What can you see *behind* me?'

The hand shot up again. 'I'm not sure, sir.'

'Not sure? You've been here two weeks, and you're still not sure? Why not?'

'I can't see, sir. You're in the way, sir.'

Mr. Merryman took an emphatic step to one side, and swept his hand in the direction of the ancient pile. 'This, boys, is Malplaquet – one of the finest eighteenth-century mansions anywhere in the world. A home for dukes, prime ministers, poets, writers, artists, and royal personages. Where people have seen Beauty in harmony with Nature and Art. And soon you will see the same. Let's begin with these sheets, the one marked "A". What do you think you're looking at?'

Johnstone's hand was first up. Merryman should have known better, but he nodded at him. The answer was rapid and totally accurate. 'Sir, it's a piece of pa . . .'

'Yes, Johnstone,' he said patiently, 'so it is, a piece of paper, and *yours* has just blown away . . . run, boy, run!'

The lesson went well in the temporary absence of one pupil. It was soon agreed that they were looking at an early print of the North Front of Malplaquet House, and the boys were asked to find similarities to the present building.

'Well spotted, Hart. Yes, the steps are still there, and the central portico . . . and those two walls extending either side.'

Another hand crept up at the back. 'Sir, those square columns are like the ones at Blenheim. Did Vanbrugh design these as well?'

Mr. Merryman beamed even more brightly than usual, and chatted with Biddle about that real possibility. Jamie Thompson scowled. '*I* knew that,' he thought. He was also annoyed that young Biddle was showing such interest in the place. It was predictable, but still annoying.

The teacher's good mood lasted until Johnstone returned clutching a soggy ball of paper, which had stopped when jumped on. 'Good, welcome back, no, don't try to unwrap it, just share with Davis. Now, who can spot the *differences* nowadays?'

Boys like Johnstone just never give up, and teachers like Merryman just keep encouraging them (it can make lessons more interesting). 'Everything then was black and white, sir, and nowadays everything here is in col . . .'

That final contribution of Johnstone was cut short by a loud cry of frustration from Merryman that, judging by its strength and speed, erupted from somewhere deep within him.

Other boys, encouraged by Johnstone's enthusiasm, gradually

made other suggestions. The most perceptive were that the women in billowy dresses were no longer walking around, two deer being chased by young men had clearly escaped, a clump of trees had simply vanished, and two old men sat by a statue were missing, presumed dead, because the print was dated 1743 and they didn't look well enough to survive another 263 years. Mr. Merryman pointed out other features that the boys had not spotted: a large lake used to be right in front of them, and a prominent equestrian statue of a regal figure on horseback was still present but much nearer the house. 'Now, boys, who can tell me why that horse is still here? Why hasn't that disappeared? Austen?'

'Because it's not a real horse, sir. It's a statue, sir. They don't move, sir.'

Merryman thought of four words: 'early retirement, pension, holidays.'

Jamie saw his chance. 'It's a statue of King George II, sir. He was the king who gave the first owner of Malplaquet a huge reward for being a successful general.' Merryman smiled in relief. 'Splendid, Thompson. Yes, Biddle?'

'But isn't it George I, sir?'

'Indeed it is, Biddle. Well done.'

Jamie was now more determined than ever to learn about the gardens and its buildings. He was also thoroughly convinced that young John Biddle, Esquire, was a nasty and arrogant piece of work who doubtless intended harm to the tiny inhabitants of Malplaquet.

Something was going to have to be done.

Julius Newbold sat in his small square bedroom, *very* fed up. The National Trust had accommodated him in one of the two flats in the Corinthian Arch. He had a couple of rooms, one above the other, on the eastern side, and another volunteer occupied those in the other block. If the two men wanted to, they could clamber up their own spiral staircases and meet on the top platform, which gave magnificent views across to Malplaquet one way and down the long avenue to Buckingham the other. But they didn't want to. Julius was wary of chatting to anybody; he was partly embarrassed by some of his facial scars that hadn't yet healed properly, and the other worker only ever said, '*Really*?' or 'I know what you mean.'

He was fed up partly because he was shivering. The recent strong winds had blown down the overhead power-line, and he was seated by his desk trying to see by the light of a candle, and trying to stay warm by the heat of the same candle. The thin wax column would have found either one of those jobs difficult; attempting to do both, it had virtually given up the struggle. The room was gloomy and cold.

Newbold was also fed up because, for weeks, he had been doing nothing but building a wall (on the inside of a ditch, and so technically known as a *ha-ha*) that was becoming as long as the one in China. This 'ha-ha' was no joke. He had slipped and slithered down the bank at least (so he reckoned) twenty times a day. He had cut himself trying to clear brambles that had been growing unchecked for years. He had spent hours – days – being miserable; hacking out broken stones from the decrepit old wall, splitting his nails and scraping his fingers on rough edges, digging out tree roots, and mixing authentic eighteenth-century cement in an authentic eighteenth-century way – by hand.

Above all, he hated it because it was hard work and he didn't like hard work, and he wasn't sure he'd seen a single Lilliputian since he'd started.

And he knew at this moment that he could no longer put off writing to Biddle.

A sudden draught blew out his only source of light and heat. 'Blast,' he muttered, and felt his way over to the dresser where he'd left the box of matches. He found it, struck a match, and as it spluttered into life he caught sight of himself in the mirror.

He instinctively recoiled. It wasn't that he was unusually ugly, although lit from below his shadowy face did have a menacing quality to it. The problem was that it wasn't him. The surgeon had done an astonishing job; nose re-shaped, chin squared, eyes lifted, lips filled, eyebrows plucked, skin stretched, bank account reduced. Even his own mother wouldn't recognize him – not that she had seen him for years anyway.

He took another look at his new image, forcing himself to imprint it on his mind and, cupping the match carefully, returned to the desk. He re-lit the candle, settled himself down with pen and paper, and began reluctantly to write.

> *To Mr. Biddle,*
> *I must first of all thank you for arranging my stay in the Arch.*
> *It is comfortable and the neighbours are fine. It is the perfect*
> *place to stay.*

He paused, remembering his previous living-quarters, a grotty tent in the Japanese Gardens. At least he was going up in the world. He continued with the lies.

> *The work is interesting and enjoyable, making me fitter and*
> *better able to patrol the grounds. The team you recommended*
> *in London were excellent and highly-skilled. They have taken*
> *years and inches off my face.*

Julius wondered if Mr. Biddle was interested in what had happened in London. Probably not. He quickly got to the point.

> *I am sorry to report no definite sightings of Lilliputians near the*
> *outer limits of Malplaquet. At least they are not trying to leave.*

Would Biddle understand this optimistic note? He wasn't sure.

> *The continuing presence of the girl in my group also suggests*
> *they are still present, and the older Thompson spends most of*
> *his free time with the old woman.*
> *I think I had a sighting of the people, but it was at a distance.*
> *Delivering fencing materials near the Copper Bottom Lake, I*
> *spotted the woman with a radio-controlled boat. Visibility was*
> *poor, but there may have been small people inside it. I was unable*
> *to approach nearer.*

Newbold didn't want to bother Biddle with the details.

> *When I have firm sightings or a closer encounter, I will immediately*
> *be in contact. I do have many plans to put into place.*
> *I have often seen John in the grounds. You will be pleased*
> *to know that he is always on his own, reading books or making*
> *notes, and he is taking great interest in his surroundings, as you*

> *required. I do not know if he has the sight.*
>
> *It would be wrong of me to mention money, as I have reported no definite good news, but any advance payment would be met with gratitude.*
>
> *Your servant as ever,*
> *Julius Newbold*

He didn't hold out much hope about this final request for money, and knew that Biddle wasn't interested in whether Julius felt grateful or not. As a rule, Biddle didn't care what people felt. Julius folded the letter into an envelope, sat back in his chair and thought more about his plans. He knew full well that Biddle wasn't going to be patient – or absent – for much longer.

'My dear Nigriff, old chap, do hang on,' puffed Thorclan, a newly demoted Rear-Admiral, desperately trying to keep up with the hurrying figure of the Permanent Grand Archivist. 'I'm very happy to come, but it would help if I knew why.'

Nigriff slowed to a halt on the path by the side of the Octagon Lake and waited for the General to catch up and regain his normal rates of breathing. 'I do apologise, but I intended to say more when we arrived. We are heading towards the Pebble Alcove.' He began to stride off again.

'I guessed as much,' panted Thorclan, still hoping for a breather. 'But why me? No water involved, I hope?'

'No water, General, but I know I can count on you.'

'Can't argue with that,' replied Thorclan. 'There are three types of people in this world, those you can count on, and those that can't count . . . or something like that.' Then the obvious question occurred to him. 'Count on me for what?' he shouted to the figure in front.

'For keeping your eyes open,' replied Nigriff over his shoulder.

Five minutes later they both stood in front of the arched alcove, with its family crest and various shapes picked out in pebbles on the inner cement walls.

'Guard duty, eh?' said Thorclan. 'So who might turn up?'

Nigriff spoke seriously. 'General, they are called the Forces of Destruction.'

'Forces of destruction?' said Thorclan calmly. 'Never heard of them; must be a new regiment.'

'Their campaign history goes back to the eighteenth century, and they are getting stronger by the day.'

'Recruiting, are they? What's their uniform?'

'No-one has ever seen them, General.'

'I know why, Nigriff, it's an old army trick – camouflage. These chaps may be clever, but they won't get past Thorclan. Now, what do you want me to do exactly?'

Nigriff breathed in slowly and deeply, feeling surprisingly nervous. 'I am going in, and I may be some time. When I return, you must tell me everything you saw – *everything*, no matter how strange or frightening.'

Thorclan caught the tone of Nigriff's voice. 'My word, you're making this sound jolly tough. Good job I'm GLOB and SCAB nowadays.' He adjusted his clothes, and made a careful visual sweep of the immediate vicinity. He couldn't see anybody totally hidden in camouflage gear, so he whispered, 'All clear, Nigriff.'

Nigriff briefly hesitated, his mind racing. The images inside the Alcove had been too erratic; some had been helpful, but Vicky had hardly seen anything, and once it hadn't worked even for Jamie. Nigriff also couldn't forget the firing of the gun – was that a warning? Nevertheless, the obligations of research and the request from the Listener decided him; he plucked up courage, gingerly stepped forward, and once inside turned to face Thorclan – who waved and gave him a confident 'thumbs up.' Nigriff glanced up anxiously at the symbols; this time lots of lines caught his eye.

The mist curtain dropped down behind him, blocking out his view. So far, so good; this was to be expected. He noticed he was no longer worried, but instead felt surprisingly safe and comfortable, as if being held, even hugged. It was a secure feeling, and reminded him of home, or of childhood. He enjoyed the sensation, and tried to savour it.

Images now appeared. Several ropes were stretched high above the ground, like a series of tightropes in parallel. People were trying to walk along them and, as they teetered and tottered, Nigriff realised with delight that he was watching Lilliput's famous rope-dancing sessions. On these occasions, politicians desiring the

King's favour had to impress him with their skill and bravery on the 'strait rope.' He recalled reading that Flimnap, the Treasurer, could dance on the rope at least an inch higher than any other Lord. Then Nigriff actually saw Flimnap himself beginning his walk, showing his dexterity – but not keeping his balance, rocking from side to side, waving his arms madly . . .

'Look out!' shouted Nigriff in warning.

'Where?' said Thorclan, turning round quickly. 'Are they here?'

Nigriff stared at the view before him – grass, bushes, a lake, and a General. The mist screen had dissolved.

Rubbing his eyes, he slowly wandered out. Thorclan was prodding the undergrowth, peering under bushes.

'Sorry, General,' said Nigriff. 'I thought I saw something.'

'Don't worry,' said Thorclan. 'Shout first and think second . . . or maybe. . . .'

Nigriff mopped his forehead. 'We can go anyway. That was long enough.'

'Long enough?' queried Thorclan. 'You just walked in, waved, and came out again!'

'But I was there for *at least* three minutes,' replied Nigriff. 'And the mist . . .'

'Mist?' queried the soldier. 'Must have missed the mist . . . no, mist have mussed . . . didn't see it,' said Thorclan. 'Definitely wasn't three minutes – sounds like a miscount. Let me explain . . .'

They began to walk alongside the lake with Thorclan outlining the finer points of the numerical system, but Nigriff wasn't really listening. He was trying to understand what had just happened; at least it was confirmation of the building being an Archive, a visual store of the Gulliver story. And perhaps it was also an Oracle, giving messages – that clue before about glasses had certainly made sense, but tight-rope walkers – what were they to do with? And how had a few minutes been condensed into a split-second? Was it like a dream, he mused, with adventures squashed into mere seconds of sleep? In fact was it nothing more than a dream?

Nigriff rejected the idea; it had felt more real and solid than that, and had touched him more deeply.

'The man's a fool,' snapped Biddle, screwing up the note and passing it to the man hobbling beside him. 'Why am I wasting so much time on him?' He wasn't expecting an answer, and his assistant knew better than to suggest one. The path alongside the old kitchen garden took a sharp left through a crumbling brick archway and abruptly stopped at the metallic door of a large green out-building, which filled up much of the walled area. Large enough to contain a tennis-court and recently built, the metal construction was single-storied and completely windowless. Biddle watched as the three keypads were punched, the heavy brass padlock removed, and the door scraped back.

'I think you'll be pleased,' said his guide, stepping on to the concrete floor and yanking a red lever high on the wall to his left. The room immediately buzzed with the influx of power, fluorescent tubes humming on, machines starting up, and pumps whirring into life. Biddle squinted in the bright light and surveyed his new laboratory.

The back half of the room was still full of cardboard boxes that were stacked together and surrounded by sheets of polythene, discarded bindings and splintered lengths of wood. The front part, by contrast, seemed finished, and frankly was very impressive.

The amount of stainless steel was dramatic, making the room look like a cross between a spotless kitchen in a top-class hotel and a hi-tech pet shop (but without any pets). Shining lengths of metal worktop and hard grey cupboards. Rows of cages that normally would contain rats. Anonymous machines with green lights and numbers blinking. Clear plastic food boxes, with labels like 'X3a' and 'Y2x,' on open steel racks. Three computers, files, and notepads. And finally a line of white coats, hanging to the right of two deep sinks. They completed the feel of grim and sterile perfection.

'Good,' said Biddle sharply. 'As I wanted. Its first guests will love it.'

It wasn't always easy for Vicky to keep an eye on the men because at times they were sent off to different parts of the garden. Late one afternoon, for example, she was totally on her own, driving the tractor and trailer along the main avenue out of Malplaquet, thumping over the two speed bumps, and heading towards the Oxford Bridge.

Trundling on her noisy and juddering way, she smiled at the top of the ski-slope of a road below her. It was amazing how many drivers took the hump-backed bridge at speed to see how well their cars would takeoff. The gouges in the tarmac on the far side showed how badly most of them landed. Vicky knew there was no chance of such drama in her present lumbering vehicle.

Once over the bridge, she parked on the verge next to the pile of logs that had been left for her to collect. A tree had blown over in the recent high winds, and although some of the roots were still half-buried, leaving it a horizontal version of its former self,;some branches had required serious pruning with a chain-saw. The men had had their fun, and Vicky had been sent to tidy up afterwards.

It was while she was doing the work, gloved hands picking up each freshly-sawn and sawdusted lump, that she had an eerie feeling of being watched. She cast her eyes around occasionally, thinking she would spot one of her colleagues, or perhaps a boy from the school fishing on the bank (or even possibly TQS), but she really did seem totally on her own. She began to feel uneasy, and hurled the last few logs on quickly and untidily.

That was one reason why two fell off when she drove away; the other reason was stalling the engine. At any rate, the pieces hit the road with a double 'clump.'

And at that exact moment she heard a voice behind her.

It said, 'Oops!'

A male voice, deep, and gruff. Nothing more than that one word.

Oops.

Then silence.

To her credit, Vicky looked behind immediately, hoping that someone was playing a trick on her. But there was still no sign of anybody. She stepped down off the tractor, walked back, and replaced the fallen items in the trailer, her eyes keenly scanning round.

What happened next made her feel very stupid when she thought about it afterwards, and she was glad that nobody had been there to see it.

It was when she saw the face. She literally did jump.

It was a face that she had seen many times, hundreds of times before, because it was made of stone, carved on one of the bridge's urns.

Except that this time it seemed to have some life in it.

It was hard to say what exactly – perhaps a twinkle in its piecing eyes, or maybe a sense of thought in its heavy forehead. But Vicky was no longer in any doubt as to where that one spoken word had come from – and she wasn't in any doubt as to where she was now going. Back up the hill towards Malplaquet as fast as the tractor would go, which of course wasn't as fast as she would have liked.

And she didn't care in the slightest when the first speed-bump dislodged the same two logs.

She wasn't stopping for anything – or *anyone*.

8 : Looking for an Answer

'Why didn't you *say* you'd seen him so much?' shouted Jamie at his younger brother. They were arguing on the upstairs landing.

'I didn't have to,' replied Charlie indignantly. 'He's just another friend. I've got *loads* . . . unlike some people . . .'

'Don't be *stupid*,' said Jamie, getting crosser. 'I've got lots as well.'

'Right . . ,' said Charlie. 'Which is why you spend so much time at Granny's. Of course – silly me.'

'You *still* should have told me. I'd no idea you'd been to his house.'

'That's because you're never around. And why shouldn't I go there?'

'None of your business,' replied Jamie, tight-lipped. 'Why should I tell you?'

'Fine,' said Charlie, bluntly, 'so why should I tell *you*?'

'What's going on up there?' asked Dad from below. 'Sort it out.'

Jamie stomped into his bedroom. The Biddles living nearby was a real pain. It was bad enough the young one being at the school and finding out lots about the gardens, but Charlie being involved made things much worse. The father and son were being far more devious than he had anticipated.

Charlie was intrigued. He'd never known his brother have such strong feelings over a harmless piece of information. In fact, that was it exactly, *strong feelings*! Charlie saw it all in a flash. John Biddle was *obviously* a long-lost good friend – a *really* good friend – of this Maria that Jamie fancied. Which meant that Jamie was incredibly jealous of this boy, who had suddenly turned up and knew just as much about the gardens. The newcomer had also impressed Maria – who was delighted that he'd moved here.

Charlie felt pleased with himself. His theory made complete sense, fitting the evidence *perfectly*. Furthermore, not only had he worked out Jamie's big secret, but he had also uncovered more information that would be worth plenty.

Things were looking highly promising.

'This Provincial Assembly hasn't come a moment too soon,' said Jamie. 'There's so much happening at Malplaquet.'

'I could not agree more,' nodded Nigriff, as they finally neared the Gothic Temple. Other PRs were making their way up the hill, some on the track from the direction of the Palladian Bridge, others through the longer grass from Cascadia or the Grecian Valley. 'But there may be awkward questions. Let us hope the *new* Listener can keep order as capably as Vingal.'

'A new one?' asked Jamie. 'Who is it?'

'Swartet,' said Nigriff.

'Man or woman?'

'Of course,' replied Nigriff, puzzled. 'What is the alternative – a rabbit?'

'No,' said Jamie. 'I mean – what sex is this person?'

'Female,' said Nigriff. 'As usual.'

'As usual?'

'Years of experience have taught us, sir, that women make the best Listeners. Although, many moons ago, a proposal was put forward that men might also be considered for the position. Unfortunately, the male PRs missed the crucial vote.'

'They missed the vote?'

'Yes,' said Nigriff. 'They weren't listening.'

The session began innocently enough. Yehvar (Grecian) reminded the Representatives that, with autumn upon them, they must encourage their people to stockpile provisions for the cold months ahead.

'Don't rely upon the squirrels for a well-balanced diet,' he urged. 'Last winter my family made that mistake. We lived off nut loaf, nut cake, nut roast, nut burgers, nut cutlets, and fried nuts. We had boiled, stewed, mashed and casseroled nuts. Nuts on nuts for breakfast, half a nut with groundnut coffee for elevenses, nutspread on nut bread at lunch, and nut custard for pudding. As a special treat we once had fruit and nut chocolate – but without the fruit and chocolate. Drove me . . . er, nuts.'

The PRs took copious notes, wanting to avoid a similar fate.

Chamklab (Cascadian) then proposed, 'Early Swimming in the Eleven-Acre.'

'What does "early" mean?' asked Thorclan (Grecian). 'Before breakfast?'

'What does "swimming" mean?' asked Nigriff (Elysian). 'Getting wet?'

Swartet wisely insisted on an immediate vote, and 52.34% placed one hand on their noses. Nigriff cunningly placed his free hand on Thorclan's nose, in an ancient and legally correct move (a 'paired nostril') that counted double. It caused much interest, being a political device not seen for many moons.

It was now Nigriff's turn, requested by Swartet to report on his research. Polite applause accompanied his walk to the centre of the rug. Many PRs respected him as the new Permanent Grand Archivist, and, to be fair, he had also played an important part in preventing the kidnap a few weeks ago. He cleared his throat.

'Honourable PRs, there have been dramatic changes in Malplaquet, especially our increasing visibility to humans. Our finest minds are seeking an explanation, and I have to inform you of our current conclusions. Initial research suggests that close proximity to the temples is a major factor.'

'Hang on, Nigriff,' said one PR (Sleydorn, Palladian), rising to his feet. 'Are you saying we're more likely to be seen if we're near the temples?'

'I am afraid so,' said Nigriff.

'This is utterly *ridiculous*. Many of us *live* in them. How can we stay away from them?' He looked around at his fellow PRs. A few cries of 'Shame!' could be heard.

'I know that. So do I. I'm sorry. We need to be extremely vigilant.'

'Never used to be a problem,' grumbled the PR. 'My people won't like this in the slightest.'

Nigriff tried to defend himself. 'You have my sympathy, but I am only reporting on recent findings.' He looked across at Jamie, who nodded as if to say, 'Go for it.' He consulted his notes. 'You may recall that Vingal asked me to study further the Pebble Alcove, because our Guide, Jamie Thompson, claimed to have seen images from our history there. In the interests of research, I recently became a guinea-pig.'

An elderly PR (Sneaten, Cascadian) stuck his finger in his right ear, fiddled around a bit, pulled out a large lump of something, and said to his neighbour, 'That's better – I thought he said he'd become a guinea-pig.'

'That's right,' came the reply, 'he did.' Sneaten, without warning, rammed his finger in his neighbour's ear, and started to twist it about.

Nigriff carried on. 'I must inform you that the Alcove is *undoubtedly* transmitting visual images – to be precise, records from our past.' He waited for a reaction. Narrag (Palladian) raised his hand. 'Has that happened to you, Nigriff?'

The Archivist nodded. 'Twice recently.'

'Was anybody with you?'

'The second time – General Thorclan.' Everyone looked at the soldier.

Swartet spoke up. 'General, could you tell us what you saw when Nigriff became a guinea . . . entered the Alcove.'

Thorclan looked uneasy, darting his eyes from her to Nigriff to Jamie and back again. 'Of course, I . . . um . . . I saw him . . . well, he went into the Alcove.'

'And?' said Swartet. 'After that?'

Thorclan paused, and mumbled something.

Swartet had missed his reply. 'I'm sorry, you must speak up.' Sneaten shoved his fingers in both his own ears, giving them a thorough boring.

Thorclan again hesitated, his forehead shiny with sweat, then announced reluctantly. 'He came out.'

'I'm sure he did,' said Swartet. 'After all, he stands here before us. He is no longer there. But, in the time *between* his entry and exit, precisely *what* did you see?'

Thorclan looked at Nigriff, and held up his hands as if to say, 'what can I do?' He stared back at Swartet. 'Personally, I saw nothing, but that's not to say . . .'

'Thank you, General, most helpful. Please resume your seat.' He shuffled back. 'Nigriff, do you wish to speak further?'

Still trying to show that there was some sort of vital link, Nigriff tried to point out the similarity in outline between Malplaquet and the island in their myths. Sadly, it wasn't a clever move.

'*Another* myth,' said Sneaten, 'says we originated from a primordial fried egg cooked on the back of an asthmatic turtle and, now that I think about it, the shape of our world *is* a bit like . . .'

'There's also one about a cosmic potato,' said another. 'I think it looks more like that.'

'Nigriff, do I understand you correctly?' said Swartet. 'You're claiming our old stories about a distant island are literally true – that it actually existed? That we didn't begin with the Great Divergence from the model city?'

'Yes, Madam,' replied Nigriff. 'Those are my firm beliefs.' His words were met with sniggers. He stood his ground. 'I have further evidence; it concerns the figure that we have for many moons threatened naughty children with.'

'The Biddleman?' asked Swartet.

Nigriff nodded. 'This is the most alarming part of my report,' he said. 'Again, he *really* did exist, in our actual history. He was a sea-captain, who kidnapped a group of our ancestors from Lilliput. I am sorry to say that one of his despicable descendants wants to recapture us. He has already placed his son in Malplaquet School.'

The PRs were unsure whether to laugh or be serious. A hand went up. 'What does this son of our great enemy look like? Like his awful father – fire flashing from his fingertips, eyes the size of dinner plates, clawed feet?'

'No,' said Nigriff. 'He's like any other schoolboy, but often wanders round Malplaquet by himself, with a book, making notes.'

'Oo-er,' said Warlek in mock fright. 'He sounds really nasty.' The sniggers could be contained no longer and the taunts began. 'Where does the Biddleman live? Dadford? Buckingham? Surely not Milton Keynes?'

'Chackmore,' replied Nigriff. 'In the Manor. A simple check will confirm that the new owner is called Biddle.'

The place became merry. Members introduced themselves as, 'Mr. Biddle of Chackmore Manor, you might have heard of me,' and others hid in mock fright. Someone yelled, 'He's *behind* you!' and another shouted, 'The Incarnation of All Evil living in the High Street will wreck Chackmore's house prices!'

Swartet motioned to Nigriff to sit down; he asked for one last word. He spoke firmly and steadily.

'My fellow Representatives, however low your opinion of my findings, I should mention that the Headteacher of the Elysian school is kindly allowing me to explain this theory of our origins to the children. Just as today, I will suggest to them that we are really citizens of *another* country, Lilliput, the home of our forebears.'

'The home of the four bears?' asked a sleepy Grecian PR, Deyuk, startled by his final words. 'Is it next to the home of the *three* bears? In the woods?'

'And, Nigriff,' said another, 'did you eat the four bears' porridge? Keep hold of your chair, Madam Listener, he'll want to sit in it next!' The laughter went on and on. Nigriff sat down, humiliated, but he had warned them; that was all he could do.

The session finished with the Listener mentioning the forthcoming School Firework Display. 'The bell by Bell Gate will be rung as usual. Try to remain calm. If you do emerge from hiding, you *might* consider Nigriff's theory about the revealing effect of the temples; that of course is entirely *your* decision.'

The PRs filed out the door, Jamie standing to one side. Thorclan walked over to Nigriff. 'I'm sorry, old boy,' he said ruefully. 'I didn't know what else to say.'

'It is not your fault,' said Nigriff. 'You spoke truly and honourably.'

'To be brutally honest with you, I don't know what to think,' said Thorclan. 'If you'd said all this a few moons ago, my lads would have drilled it out of you. But now . . . now I'm not so sure. I was *there* when Smelly tried to kidnap Yenech again. A boy called Biddle *has* moved into the Manor. We've "gained the capital". And the temples *are* doing odd things to us. Something really *is* going on.'

'What's going on is what is *coming*, General,' said Nigriff. 'It's the *Empire*. At last. The fact that we are talking so amicably is one sign; we are becoming *one* people. I would be ashamed to admit to you my previous opinion of Grecians.'

'Wild. Uncivilised. Savages,' replied Thorclan. 'Don't worry, I knew. And it's true anyway!' he added with a chuckle and a broad grin, clapping his hands on his friend's shoulders. 'Nigriff, there's lots I don't understand – the Alcove, disappearing islands, and almost everything about Yenech – but I'm sure of *one* thing. You've *changed*. All this Lilliput stuff *might* be true. Anyway,' he continued, 'I used to think badly of you as well.'

'Really?'

'Oh, yes. I thought you were a boring, arrogant, opinionated academic with no physical abilities. But it's not true.' He paused for effect. 'You're not boring.'

Thorclan laughed out loud, a warming and comforting laugh. Nigriff joined in, and Jamie happily watched them wander off down the hill.

'Right, gentlemen,' announced Mr Davies, who was coaching hockey to the new boys, 'drills over, time for a bit of a game.'

'At last,' thought Jamie. 'This is kid's stuff.' He'd become increasingly frustrated at the basic tuition that lots of other boys needed – like how to hold the stick, how to hit the ball, how to pass it to another person. For years, Jamie had been playing street-hockey with Charlie on their roller-blades, and he was finding it too easy to transfer those skills to Astroturf. His only enjoyment so far had been seeing how inept John Biddle was. Unused to wielding any sort of sports equipment, the boy was also wearing over-sized shirts and shorts, and was ungainly and awkward when trying to run.

'Line up in alphabetical order,' instructed Mr. Davies, with his usual mathematical sense of order, watching them check each other's names and straggle into a line. 'Team A,' he said, dividing it down the middle, 'keep your blue shirts, and Team B pick up those green bibs. Sort out your own positions. We haven't got time to get the keepers kitted up, so we'll play rush goalies, and no *long* shots at goal – you can only score by pushing the ball in.'

Jamie was delighted to be playing against Biddle, and to have Lake, known to be a good attacker, on his own team. For the first ten minutes, Jamie humiliated his opponent as often as possible, dribbling round him, doing nifty one-twos with Lake that left Biddle looking foolish and pathetic, and once managing a neat shoulder-charge that Jamie was annoyed to get blown-up for. At least it left the boy sprawling on the rough surface. 'Rugby's *next* term, Thompson,' shouted the coach. 'Just concentrate on your ball skills – and stop showing off by playing one-handed!'

'Yes, sir, sorry, sir,' replied Jamie. He hung back a bit after that, and had to endure the sight of the teacher encouraging the more useless boys. 'Well done!' he shouted, when one boy actually hit the ball. 'Top man, Biddle!' he yelled, when John trotted over to the side-line and stopped the ball from slowly rolling out.

Jamie had had enough; it was time for some direct action. He had decided in his own mind that this was probably another one of those battles, mentioned in Pope's poem, that as the Guide he was meant to be fighting.

He chose the moment of conflict very carefully. He waited until both he and Biddle had a chance of reaching the ball, and were likely to arrive at the same time – John from three metres away, Jamie from twice that distance. The collision was inevitable, but made worse by Jamie cunningly thrusting his stick at the last minute between his opponent's legs, causing the boy to cartwheel over and land awkwardly on the unforgiving surface. Mr. Davies blew the whistle and ran over. 'Dangerous play, Thompson, I told you to use *both* hands. Bring me the ice-pack and then go and sit down by the pavilion.' The coach bent down to check for any damage on John, who was moaning and rubbing his leg.

Jamie wandered off the pitch, pleased with his efforts. 'Forces of Darkness?' he thought to himself. 'I don't think so. That'll show them.'

Granny was seated in her favourite wing armchair with the high arms, useful for leaning on when she was sewing and making clothes. She was surrounded by a sea of squares of material, reels of cotton, the occasional half-dressed doll, scissors, tape measures and sketches, and was thinking hard.

It had been a remarkable few months – exciting, but also wor-rying. The exciting part was that the Guide, her favourite young friend, was slowly but surely fulfilling Pope's old prophecy. He was uniting and leading the people. The Empire *was* becoming stronger. And there was an odd link between the shape of Malplaquet and Lilliput, which had really surprised her. Jamie was now even talking about the temples somehow transmitting some sort of energy from the island. The fact that Lilliput no longer existed didn't seem at all to worry him; he had unbounded optimism, the confidence of youth that all would turn out well.

A number of things, however, were worrying Granny. The Lilliputians were being frustratingly difficult about accepting their long and glorious history. Nigriff had set out his arguments with the Academic Board *and* an Assembly of PRs, and both still thought that their history began with the Great Divergence from the Japanese Gardens. At least he still had another chance with the children in the Elysian school; perhaps some of them might listen. She recalled various conversations with the Lilliputians as a young girl, when the people were so proud of their heritage, appreciating their unique nature and character. Nowadays most were oddly content with thinking they were no more than accidental blots on the landscape.

Her eyes moistened.

Then she thought of the danger they were in. She needed no convincing about the threat of Biddle. He had undoubtedly inherited his ancestor's cunning and viciousness, a self-centred determination to exploit these tiny people for his own ends. Jamie had described to her the nasty side of the son as well. She had asked what John looked like, but Jamie hadn't wanted to talk about him, and she hadn't pushed the matter. The boy and his father were obviously bent on evil – and now were living only about a mile away.

She suddenly felt very upset, and put down her needle and thread in her lap. Why was she bothering to make clothes for people that might soon be – well, what might happen to them? Captured and taken away? Put in a museum? Experimented upon? She bit her lip to stop the tears. What was to be done? She did believe in Jamie, in his bravery and determination, but the truth was that he was still only a very young man. The TQS team had worked miracles before, but frankly they had been extremely fortunate. Then there was Vicky, busy with her A-Levels and being a part-time Volunteer. That only left her, a short-sighted old lady, armed with plenty of memories, intermittent rheumatism, and an under-powered Golf Trolley.

It didn't add up to much. They were going to need far more help. She adjusted a pottery figure on the window-sill, and stared out, blinking and stroking away a couple of tears that threatened to be the start of a real weep.

Her attention was caught by a slight movement at ground level in the yard. At first it was so quick she thought her eyes were playing tricks on her, but when it happened again, she knew she wasn't imagining it.

To one side of her gatepost, half-hidden amongst her collection of pots, sat her favourite small stone lion. She had bought it years ago in an auction in town. It was seated on its haunches, one of its front paws resting on an upright shield. Jamie's Dad said it was the symbol of the Italian city of Florence. It always looked proud, even regal, but now . . . now it was looking incredibly alert, even *waking up*.

To Granny's great shock, it began shaking its head slowly from side to side, its mane rippling with the movement, and then yawned in a slow-motion way. This all lasted only a few moments but, after a pause, it did it again, and this time with more energy, and for longer.

Finally, as if nothing had happened, it returned to being just a stone lion permanently guarding her plant pots.

Granny watched it for a few minutes more, trying to come to terms with what her eyes had just seen. Then she left her seat, walked outside and inspected the lion from every angle.

It certainly *looked* cold and hard. She held out her hand cautiously above the sculpture, before tentatively placing it on the animal's head. Nothing happened. It wasn't alive; it *was* just a statue, a garden ornament.

But then from somewhere deep within, her hand felt a low vibration, little more than a murmur.

The lion was purring.

Granny quickly snatched back her hand and stepped away. This was very alarming, although she was partly pleased that a lion, costing only five pounds, was turning out to be so much more than just a stone object. Nevertheless, she was also uneasy and frankly scared, feeling exactly like she did when she had first realized that the Pebble Alcove really did contain mysterious powers. There was more, far more, to this garden than she had ever realised, and it was all very unsettling.

She tried to think about it logically as best she could. What was causing all this? Nigriff kept on warning them about the opposing Forces in the garden, especially those of 'Destruction.' Could this awakening lion be a sign that the 'Forces of Restoration' were gathering their strength as well?

She hoped, for the sake of the people of Lilliput, that it *was* such a sign.

In fact she hoped that it was more than a sign.

She hoped it was a promise.

9 : Families, Posts, and Statues

'Would you like a lift?' asked Granny. Driving on her GT through Elysium, she'd caught up with a boy struggling with an armful of files, a large sports bag – and a very pronounced limp.

John Biddle wouldn't normally have accepted such an offer, but he was tired, his leg was hurting, and this old lady did seem genuinely concerned. She was also driving an electric buggy, and he really fancied a go in it. Saying, 'Yes, please,' was easy.

'Presumably you're going to Chackmore?' she said. 'You'd never make it to Buckingham.'

'That's right,' said John. 'Chackmore.'

'I can only take you to the Corinthian Arch, I'm afraid – the battery's a bit low. Dump your things in the back, and hop in – I mean, jump . . . well, you know what I mean.' John settled down in the front seat, and relaxed immediately, relieved at being able to take the weight off his foot.

'Sports injury?' asked Granny. John just nodded. She sensed that he didn't want to talk about it, or anything else for that matter, so she let him enjoy the ride, and was amused when he soon asked, 'Does this go any faster?'

'They might be bringing out a new Coupé version soon,' she said, 'but you do get attached to these. And if I went any faster, I wouldn't see the gardens.'

'They *are* lovely,' said John. 'Do you live near them?'

'Practically *in* them,' replied Granny. 'In fact, just round here.' They drove out through Bell Gate, and she nodded at her cottage as they trundled past.

'I thought so,' said John. 'I saw you here once. You were talking to some children on horses.'

'I knew your face was familiar,' said Granny. 'Have you just started at the school?'

'Yes,' he said, 'this term.'

'I'm sure there are one or two others in Chackmore who've started as well. I've known one boy for years – have you met Jamie Thompson yet?'

John hesitated. 'Yes . . . I was playing hockey with him today.'

'Oh good,' she said. 'Chackmore's not that big a place – you probably live quite near him. Which is your house?'

'We've just moved to the village,' said John, confirming a suspicion in Granny's mind that had been developing as they crawled up the dirt track. She wasn't at all surprised when he stated that 'We live in the Manor.'

To her credit, Granny kept up her amicable chat with him until the drop-off point, although it wasn't too difficult. John seemed a good-natured boy, and it was far harder to work out how he could be the son of the enemy of the Lilliputians, and also why Jamie had such a poor opinion of the lad. As John slowly wandered down the long slope, Granny sat for a while in her buggy, trying to make sense of it all.

The incredibly important man from the Head Office of the National Trust was thoroughly enjoying his day out at Malplaquet. He had been driven around in an electric kart (waving majestically at the ordinary people en route), been pleasingly wined and dined at the poshest restaurant in Buckingham, and was now lecturing the staff and volunteers in the newly refurbished 'Education, Awareness and Information Exchange Resource Facility' (formerly known as the Lecture Room).

'Let me outline two initiatives, inceptioned and strategified in a recent policy momentum gear-shift at Head Office,' he enthused, knowing from experience this would whip up his audience into a frenzy of corporate excitement. 'Firstly, we've been discussing with our foremost key stakeholders an old post which has fallen into disuse at Malplaquet.'

The Head Gardener was astonished; one of his fence posts had fallen over, and *he* didn't know about it but Head Office did? And who were these four, most key fencing people he'd been talking to? 'The new post's name, reflecting the centrality of the position, is *Customer Relations Adviser and Transport Logistics Consultant.*'

The Head Gardener was now even more bewildered. The new fence-post had been given a *name*? And a name like that?

The lecture continued. 'The primary target is consumer awareness, to foster appropriate relations and implement a policy of equality of opportunity and information, regardless of age, gender, race, religion, ethnicity and manubalance . . .'

'Sorry,' interrupted Vicky, her right hand in the air, 'what was that last word?'

'Has 'manubalance' not yet arrived in the shires?' asked Mr. Head Office, looking at the blank faces. 'It's a helpful concept much used in the metropolis. Discrimination against left-handed people has been a long-standing and major social injustice. The Trust has now issued a public apology for its historic prejudice, and is at the forefront of attempts to combat this heinous and arrogant attitude.'

'I see,' said Vicky, wishing she had put up her left hand and rightly feeling very conspicuous, prejudiced and guilty.

'The appointed person will identify and prioritize organisational issues, direct positive solutions and outcomes to logistical problems, remove barriers and improve access for vehicular transport, highlight pedestrians' basic needs and rights, and . . .'

'Hang on,' interrupted Vicky, 'are you talking about cars and visitors?'

'A crude description,' said the suit. 'The cycling community would feel . . .'

'They don't feel anything,' said Vicky. 'That's why they ride those things. Tell me, when this post *was* last in place, exactly what was it called?'

'My dear, we have rejected narrow and out-moded terminology; we no longer merely call people *Car Park Attendants.*'

'Ooh, I could do that,' called one man. 'I'd love to organise parking and chat to visitors. I hoped it was, when you mentioned barriers and access.'

That positive outcome pleased everybody and considerably lightened the atmosphere, although Head Office Man mentally noted that the new appointee would benefit from a series of Awareness-Raising Workshops. He outlined his second initiative. 'We've taken on board the desirability of launching a new project, as incentivisation levels are declining due to excessive wall-restructuring programmes.'

'Too right, mate,' grumbled one worker, making a quick and accurate translation. 'We want to do summat else rather than just build walls.'

'Point taken,' agreed the speaker. 'So the Head Gardener will now launch and roll out the new enterprise.' Their man duly launched himself and rolled out.

'Mornin.' We're going to build a Duck Decoy down on the Eleven-Acre . . .'

'Mum, can John come in for a bit?'

'Of course, but Jamie's not around, he's having tea at Granny's again.' Charlie was relieved; there was no way that Jamie would have wanted John in the house. Mum was much more welcoming.

'Hello, John, come in. How are things at the Manor? Is all the work finished?'

'I think the inside's done, but some new buildings outside need finishing.'

'Has your Dad moved in yet?'

'He came last week, but I haven't seen much of him.'

Mrs Thompson decided not to delve any further. 'So what are you two going to do?' she asked Charlie.

'John's doing a project about Malplaquet, about famous things that have happened there. I'm going to help him with some ideas.'

John held up a large book with stiff red covers. 'I'm doing this, *Mistress Masham's Repose*. It's a story about Malplaquet.'

'Super. Off you go then, and don't go in Jamie's bedroom.'

'Wouldn't dream of it,' said Charlie.

Once they were gone, Mr Thompson's head appeared round the sitting-room door. 'I'm not sure how good an influence that boy is on Charlie.'

'What do you mean?'

'Well, just how academic is he? You've got the chance to do some fascinating research on important events, and he chooses a children's book! He could have done Queen Victoria's stay in 1845, or maybe that 1920 dredging of the lakes when they found the second Duke's coach and six footmen preserved in the mud, or in 1956 when his Royal Highness, the Crown Prince Airohine III of Nigeria, was invited to plant a commemorative tree and he planted an old groundsman instead. Any of those could be excellent projects . . . but a *children's story*?'

'Personally, I think he's made a good choice,' said his wife.

Upstairs Charlie and John were lying down, flicking through the book. 'I've seen this before,' said Charlie. 'Jamie got one from his girlfriend – you know, Maria.'

'Maria?' queried John. 'Who's Maria?'

Charlie groaned silently. Not *another* one being awkward, he thought; these two boys are so difficult. He explained the situation. 'Maria is Jamie's girlfriend – at least she *used* to be until . . .' He paused. 'Until she became your . . . your . . . friend.'

'I haven't got a friend called Maria,' said John. 'I hardly know any girls. The only Maria I know is the one in this book.' Charlie felt frustrated; adolescent boys obviously liked to hide the truth. However, he didn't want to spoil his growing friendship with John. 'Okay, whatever. What are you going to do with this story?'

'I thought I'd make a large poster – parts of the first chapter, some copies of the drawings, and bits of information about the author, T.H. White.'

'Sounds fine, but I've just had a brilliant idea,' said Charlie. 'Put in a few photos of the grounds – in fact, even *better*, some photos of Lilliputians.'

'They're not real,' said John.

'Seriously?' said Charlie in feigned surprise. 'Not to worry – my Granny has got this collection of dolls that would do. She'll let us borrow a couple.'

John liked the idea, and they sifted through the book to find some scenes they could one day photograph with their models.

The rigours of the school-day over, afternoon tea at Granny's was always a welcome stopping-off point for Jamie on the way home. He loved hearing her tales of living in the mansion as a little girl, and of the enormous grounds (before they were open to the public) when it was like her own private wilderness, with decaying temples glimpsed through branches and undergrowth.

But the pair didn't always have a totally friendly chat, and indeed today Granny got quite cross with Jamie. She mentioned that she'd recently met John Biddle, and had even given him a lift. That annoyed Jamie, but Granny was unrepentant. 'He was *limping*,' she said. 'The poor boy could hardly walk.'

'Serve him right,' said Jamie. 'He shouldn't be so pathetic at hockey. And Pope says we're meant to be fighting the Biddles anyway.'

'Was that injury *your* fault?' she asked.

'Not exactly, it was an accident. But a *lucky* accident.'

'Pope's prophecy says nothing about going mad with a hockey stick,' she said. 'And John does seem a nice boy.'

'Looks can be deceptive,' replied Jamie. 'He's more clever than you think.'

'Thank you, Master Jamie,' said Nigriff, walking in through the open door. 'You're too kind.'

Nigriff was eventually persuaded that they hadn't been discussing *him*, and he was asked to settle their difference of opinion about young Biddle. His judgement was that John certainly needed watching carefully, and it wouldn't matter if Granny bumped into him again. Which was exactly what Jamie *shouldn't* do.

Granny suddenly changed the subject. 'I've got to talk over something with you all, so I've asked Vicky to pop in,' she said. 'But I might as well tell you two now anyway.' She paused before carrying on. 'It's really odd. You know my stone lion?'

'Florence?' said Jamie.

'The stone lion is called Florence, Madam?' asked Nigriff.

'No,' said Granny. 'It's like a famous one in the city of Florence. Anyway, the other day it *moved* – yawned – shook its head. And purred when I touched it.'

'Cool!' said Jamie.

'Hmm, interesting,' said Nigriff.

'Is that all?' said Granny. 'One of my garden ornaments comes to life, and all you can say is "cool" and "hmm, interesting"? Nothing more than that?'

'I might add,' said Nigriff, 'that it merits further investigation. And perhaps it is not unexpected. Consider; if buildings warm up, or transmit incidents from their history, if pebbles can produce living pictures . . . then there is Reason in a stone lion moving.'

'And it has happened to me as well,' said Jamie.

'When?' asked Granny quickly. 'With that lion?'

'No, not that,' said Jamie. 'Other things. Twice.'

'*Twice*?' asked Granny, astonished.

Jamie nodded, rather sheepishly. 'The first one was ages ago. Remember when Nigriff first took me round the four – okay, three – provinces? In Elysium, I watched the reflections of the Worthies' heads, and *they* were moving, talking to each other.'

'And you didn't mention it?' said Granny.

'I wasn't completely sure, and I thought you'd say I was crazy, and that I couldn't be your assistant.'

'Intriguing,' said Nigriff. 'I have often wondered about those heads. When walking past, I have felt *watched*, and once I believe I heard Shakespeare say, "There proceeds Nigriff, the great man of letters." I *may* be mistaken, he could have said . . .'

'Hello, my dear, how are you?' interrupted Granny. 'Come in, there's a pot just made.'

'Hi everyone, sorry I'm late.' Vicky flopped in a chair, dropping her bag.

'Flapjack?'

'Love one,' came the reply. 'But why are you lot looking so serious?'

Granny poured the tea. 'Vicky, when you came through the gate, did that little stone lion out there *do* anything?'

'The one by your plants?' Granny nodded.

Vicky looked puzzled, and then smiled. 'Funnily enough, now you mention it – it did say 'hello,' but nothing else.'

'Really?' said Nigriff, who wasn't always good at spotting sarcasm.

'No,' said Vicky. 'Joke. Sorry. Long day.'

Granny told her about her experiences with the statue; Jamie repeated his first story and then explained about the rearing horse in the Marble Saloon when they gained the capital, and Nigriff added his thoughts. Vicky listened with interest. 'Okay, let's forget what I just said – I *do* know what you mean about being watched, and faces and everything. I was down by the Oxford Bridge the other day, and I'm sure a face on one of the urns moved slightly. In fact, I think it spoke as well. Not that I've told anyone of course.'

'Hmm, interesting,' said Nigriff. 'What did it say?'

'Not a lot,' replied Vicky. 'Just "oops". But at the time it was really scary.'

There was some sympathy for Vicky, and they accepted that they would have to keep their ears and eyes open, and keep each other informed of other occurrences. Nigriff also took the opportunity to make a big announcement. 'It has been on my mind for some time, but as of this moment I'm stepping down as a member of the Thompson Quad Squad, in order to spend more time researching Malplaquet and Lilliput. It has become increasingly difficult to juggle *both* demands, and I fear it has badly affected my attendance at training sessions. It only remains for me to thank . . .'

'Nigriff, you've *never* been to a training session,' said Vicky.

'Which proves my point *exactly*,' said Nigriff. 'Nevertheless, I have in private been working on my fitness to bring it to the level required to *commence* training, and, sadly, precisely at the time when I am finally in prime condition, I have to make this traumatic decision. It will be hard to say goodbye to the athletic camaraderie of the squad, but I would be grateful, Miss Vicky, if you could express my regrets to Yenech, and my hope that he finds a comparable replacement in the very near future.'

'It won't be easy for him to find someone like you,' said Vicky, and Nigriff took that as a compliment – as she had assumed he would.

'Still building the Great Wall of Malplaquet, Vicky?' asked Granny.

'Sunday was the last day for the moment,' said Vicky. 'Only half a mile to go. But we're starting on a new project soon. Head Office want a duck decoy built on the Eleven-Acre. Some new records show there was one in the late seventeenth century.'

'What's a duck decoy?' asked Jamie, imagining a plastic bird.

'It's a long tunnel of netting that helped the owner capture ducks – which ended up roasted on the dinner-table. Far better than shooting them, otherwise the guests spent the whole meal spitting out lead pellets. If they weren't careful, they could shoot the person opposite.'

'Nasty,' said Granny. 'And what about the people you're working with? Still keeping an eye on them?'

'It's hard to get to know them,' said Vicky. 'They're not exactly the strong silent types, more the *weak* silent types. I sort of know Ralph, but I didn't like the way he ran over to the rowing-boat that time. Far too interested. He bothers me the most.'

'I knew a Ralph once,' mused Granny. 'Good chap, worked on the estate. Knew it like the back of his hand. Not as nice as Herbert though, he was a real ladies' man, and as for Harry, just the way he said, 'Good Morning, Miss M,' made me feel all funny . . . talk of all the local girls, he was . . .'

There was no stopping her now.

Jedekiah Biddle, the new Lord of the Manor of Chackmore, picked up a black bishop, dragged it along his diagonal path and knocked over a small figure that was standing in the way. The fallen knight was gripped from on high and deposited at the side of the board. 'A proper attack,' he murmured. 'Pawns are too slow.'

He stood up, stretched, cracked his knuckles, and wandered over to the study window. Outside was his son with the younger Thompson boy. The visitor was patiently showing him how to throw a Frisbee, but John was simply tossing it as if playing hoop-la at a fairground stall.

'Hopeless,' thought Jedekiah, keeping well-hidden to one side of the window. 'What a waste of time.'

He retraced his steps, stopping at two cupboard doors on the left wall. He solemnly pulled them open, and stared at the fine sculpture of the man who had started it all, Captain John Biddle. Their eyes met, and for a few moments neither face moved a muscle, no eye blinked. The silence was finally broken by the living one.

'Patience, Captain,' he said, 'patience. The time *is* coming.' He continued to gaze at his ancestor, as if awaiting a response, then lifted up his hands, grasped both handles, and gently closed the doors. One deep and calming breath, and he moved further along the shelves, selecting two thick volumes. He sat down at his desk, and began to work his way through them, stopping occasionally to ponder the words.

These tomes were the family histories of the Biddles, a line that should have become rich and powerful through its knowledge of

Lilliput, but instead had been cheated of its deserved wealth. Jedekiah read again of the sea-captain, undoubtedly brave and shrewd, but weakened by an addiction to alcohol and ultimately locked away in a 'House for the Correction of the Mentally Infirm.' No-one had believed his stories of little people. Gulliver himself had denied everything once he had heard of Biddle's scheming return voyage, and had explained his own tiny animals – the sheep and cows – by means of clever scientific theories, about nature selecting random mutations (ideas that were adopted and developed in the next century by Charles Darwin, another traveller).

Only Biddle's sons had believed him; they knew a fortune lay hidden at Malplaquet, and they had tried all sorts of tricks to tease the tiny people out.

One son, James, a Landscape Consultant to the first Duke, had continually encouraged him to re-position the temples around the gardens, hoping to disturb and bring the Lilliputians out into the open. In spite of that, they had never been spotted.

Joseph, a grandson and judge, had persuaded the second Duke to build a small-scale castle in the centre of Buckingham itself, arguing that such a fortress (and handy jail) ensured that the County Courts would be held in the town, thus bringing in much revenue. Joseph's *real* hope was that this attractive fortification might lure the Lilliputians out of their usual, less secure, habitats – but to no avail.

The castle can still be seen there, but there are as yet no records of Lilliputians ever having been spotted in Buckingham High Street.

Further on in the books were the lives of Jedekiah's great grand-parents, Joram and Jocasta. The most cunning Biddles since the sea-captain, and trusted servants of the Third Duke, they had nevertheless caused his final bankruptcy by encouraging lavish hospitality and celebrations for Queen Victoria's visit. The financial ruin had virtually emptied the whole site, and the devious couple had planned to search the grounds thoroughly.

Unfortunately for them, the French Royal Family in exile had spotted the advert in the newspaper: 'Unfurnished Georgian Property, Available Now, Detached, Entrance Hall, 63 Bedrooms, 5 Dining Rooms, 11 Bathrooms, 4 Kitchens, Open Fireplaces, Stables, Off-Road Parking, Garden with New Water Feature, Open Views, countless Squirrels, and Cheap to Run. Suit Large Family or Small Army.' It was just the sort of thing they were looking for, so they had paid six months rent in advance and moved in. Security and access in the grounds became even tighter . . .

And as for the current Biddle, he reflected, as he shut the books, what had he done so far? Many, many things but two in particular.

Firstly, he had carefully befriended, secretly swindled and helpfully employed Julius Newbold, who had once worked in the grounds many years ago. Although hopelessly pathetic and incompetent, for some incomprehensible reason Newbold had that special ability, the *rare* ability which Biddle craved almost as much as money and power – that of unusual vision. The man could actually *see* the tiny people, and naturally Biddle hated him for it. Indeed, he hated himself for depending upon the wretch, but he justified it because Newbold had his uses.

Biddle's second action had involved what he himself did possess in abundance. Money.

Rejecting the old plan of *emptying* the grounds at Malplaquet, he had decided to unsettle the tiny inhabitants by increasing visitor numbers, and so had anonymously given one million pounds to kick-start the Trust's restoration programme. It had also made access easier for Newbold, and as Jedekiah glanced up at John still looking abject and hopeless, he said to himself, 'and it looks like he's the best I've got.'

He closed the volumes, returned them to their allotted place on the shelves, and briskly strode out of the room, pulling the door hard behind him. He was starting to become impatient; he had the ideas and plans – now he needed some results.

10 : Lift-Off

In the fading evening light on 5 November, a group of about fifteen Lilliputians gathered outside the back door of Granny's cottage. They included Swartet the Listener, respected academics (including Professor Malowit and Dr Yungen), Health and Safety representatives (Generec, Nettibs, and Wonats), Miliswal, the gregarious Editor of the Daily Reflector – and two PRs (Wollbind and Bodmunce) who just wanted to be seen as being there.

Standing in their midst was a young lady, Sugofern, chosen by a Select Committee to be this year's 'Bell Belle,' the one who alerts the four provinces to the imminent Malplaquet Firework Display. She was exquisitely and immaculately dressed for the occasion – sturdy boots, thick overcoat, a coiled length of rope attractively worn just off the shoulder, and round her neck a pair of ear-muffs (super-size). Granny, Jamie and Vicky were also present; for the latter two, it was their very first 'Bell-Warning,' although of course Jamie had heard the bell in July before the Picnic Fireworks.

The Listener made a fine opening speech of welcome, and Professor Malowit outlined the event's historical and cultural background. He focussed particularly on the celebrated myth of a human called Gulliver invading their country on 5 November – hence the day's powerful association with danger. The Editor dreamt up witty puns for his front page – 'sparkling speeches,' 'flashes of inspiration,' and 'a dazzling group of celebrities.' Granny just hoped they would finish before the loud noises began.

Once the ceremonies were completed on schedule, Granny picked up Sugofern, placed her on top of the garden wall, and said the traditional words: 'You are small, and the bell is big, but run like the clappers!'

Sugofern bounded along the high and narrow walkway, keeping her balance superbly and not at all daunted by the eight-foot drop on either side. Reaching the ancient bell, she unslung the coil of rope and tied one end round the central metal clapper – luckily this year there was little wind to disturb it – and retreated, playing out the rope behind her. One metre back, she fitted the ear-muffs, looked down at the 'dazzling group,' received the nods of approval, and yanked hard for all her might, again and again. Even the three humans put their hands over their ears, and Jamie saw that the reverberations were sending noticeable tremors through the Lilliputians.

The necessary task was accomplished. Throughout the grounds of Malplaquet, tiny people were taking precautions for the forth-coming display. Shutters were being bolted across windows, pet shrews and voles brought inside, buckets filled with water for any stray incendiaries, and people downwind (Grecians this year) were donning smoke-masks and sticking tape across the surrounds of doors and windows.

Bonfire Night is an evening you don't look forward to if you are only six inches high.

Jamie was often thinking, and of course worrying, about the Lilliputians, but during his lessons at school he could usually forget about them for the moment. At least he could as long as none of them actually turned up in the classroom . . . .

It all happened so quickly. One minute he was simply leaning down by the side of his desk and reaching inside his bag for his pencil-case, and the next he was sat transfixed, holding out in front of him an immobile General Thorclan, dressed in full green and brown camouflage gear. The old soldier was looking at him with a definite twinkle in his eye, as if to say, 'I bet you didn't expect to find *me* here, did you?'

Jamie gulped. Thorclan gave him a subtle wink.

A definite sniggering began from the boys behind and either side of Jamie. The teacher, who had been in full flow at the front, stopped in mid-sentence, aware that there was a new centre of interest in the room. 'Something *funny* going on back there?' he asked, staring in their general direction.

'No, sir,' volunteered one boy, hardly able to contain his laugh, 'it's just that Thompson has brought his Action Man with him!'

Everybody turned round to look at Jamie, and also at the stiff figure clenched in his hand. Some couldn't resist making sarcastic comments, such as, 'Couldn't you leave your little friend behind?' and 'Sir, can we have a playtime now, like we used to have in our last school?' The teacher knew he would have to act quickly, and he strode down the aisle between the desks, towards Jamie and his Action Man.

'Right, Thompson, I'm afraid this little soldier has just been captured. Hand him over.' Jamie did nothing, but felt Thorclan stiffen in his grasp, and noticed his tiny right hand wrapping its fingers around the small dagger attached to his belt. This could turn *very* nasty; he knew there was no way that Thorclan would allow himself to be taken.

'Sir, please sir, it's not mine, it belongs to an old lady that I know, she collects dolls, I've got to give it to her after school.'

'So why are you playing with it now?'

'I wasn't, sir, I was just looking in my bag for my pencil-case, and I picked it up by mistake.'

'Just *jumped* into your hand, I suppose? A bid for freedom, perhaps?'

'No, sir, of course not, sir.'

'I think it would be best if I looked after it for the rest of the lesson. Collect it from me at the end.'

And so saying, he took the old General from Jamie, walked back to his desk and shut the figure away in one of the drawers, slamming it hard for effect to show the boys that the incident was now over and he was once more in charge. Although it was very gloomy inside, Thorclan quickly reconnoitred the new terrain and made himself comfortable amongst all the board-markers, paper-clips, envelopes, and odd bits of mathematical equipment such as protractors, calcula- tors and a pair of compasses.

In fact, it was that last item that probably explained why, at the end of the lesson, as the teacher idly reached in to pick up the captive, he withdrew his hand with a sudden yell, quickly grasped one finger in his other hand, and then began to suck it. One minute later, as the bleeding from the small but deep puncture wound was still refusing to stop, he left the room in a hurry. 'Get it yourself, Thompson,' he announced over his shoulder, 'and I don't want to see it ever again.'

'Good things, those spears,' said Thorclan, as Jamie lifted him out from his hideaway.

'They're actually compasses, General,' said Jamie.

'*Compasses*?' he replied. 'Are you sure? No wonder Yenech is always getting lost. But they do have other uses . . . The Grecian army will definitely be putting an order in.'

'Good point, General,' said Jamie, gently placing him back in his bag.

'They certainly do have,' replied Thorclan, nodding firmly, 'they certainly do.'

It had been an extraordinary few months for the Lilliputians. After the early anxieties about how Jamie's appointment had affected the provinces, they had gradually accepted him – and Vicky – as a real asset. They had known for a long time that Granny was finding it more and more difficult to be their guardian, and so recruiting two sympathetic humans was regarded as a welcome step.

The tiny inhabitants were naturally worried about their increasing visibility to humans, but their concerns had proven to be largely groundless so far, and anyway, with the summer over, it was less of a problem. The hours of daylight and numbers of visitors decreased together; on particularly damp days in the autumn Malplaquet was largely deserted apart from the volunteers – and they were usually working on a localised project, like the decoy, or putting up authentic eighteenth-century fences in an authentic eighteenth-century manner (very slowly). Even the frightening intrusion by Old Smelly was fast disappearing into the mists of time and memory, transformed into a mythical story that parents told their children – like the one about the nasty Biddleman.

One small person, however, continued to talk about that particular name as a *real* figure of history, not as a figment of their ancestors' imagination. Nigriff.

He became a minor celebrity that autumn, not only outlining his views in schools, but also appearing in articles in the popular (and unpopular) press. '*Lilliput – history or hysteria?*' was closely followed by '*Nigriff, provincial man of mystery,*' and '*Repeat after me – island, you land, he lands.*' There was even a flurry of excitement when a Deep Marsh Expedition revealed traces of foundations in the centre of the Eleven-Acre Lake, until Professor Nozna pointed out that archaeological evidence for an island did not necessarily confirm that people had ever lived on it.

Other academics also kept up their opposition; Professor Vangor contributed a perceptive piece of research describing other things he had found that didn't exist, and Dr Yungen delivered a daring lecture on Nigriff's mental state. This was his stunning conclusion.

'Thus, as I have shown, Nigriff doesn't believe in things that are *true*. Nigriff believes what he *wishes* to happen, such as an ideal homeland – what we call wish-fulfilment. Or that he *fears* might happen, such as facing a vicious enemy (fear-fulfilment). Or things that he isn't bothered about (apathy-fulfilment). My friends, all I can say is that I believe you should believe the beliefs Nigriff doesn't believe!'

His audience had been reduced to amazed silence by such extraordinary and compelling logic.

No-one could deny that a couple of Biddles were now living in Chackmore Manor, but their presence had not become a cause for alarm. Indeed, the 'Son of All Evil' (as the *Moon* newspaper was now happily calling John) was proving to be a meek and ineffectual character, who spent most of his time on his own, writing in notebooks, taking photos, or sitting looking sad and forlorn under a tree. A significant proportion of Lilliputians found it hard to accept Nigriff's assessment of either John or his family line. Even Granny was occasionally expressing doubts.

The gardeners were battening down the hatches for winter by cutting back or tying up plants, the Lilliputians were starting to feel safe even by the temples, and generally things seemed to be getting back to normal.

And that of course is precisely when you have to be particularly careful.

You are never in more danger than when you think there is nothing to be afraid of.

'Right, you two, stay in the field behind Venus. *Don't* make a nuisance of yourselves, and don't frighten the animals with it.'

'Trust us, Dad,' said Charlie. 'We'll be fine.'

'Hmm,' replied Mr Thompson, hardly reassured but reluctant to say anything in front of John Biddle. 'Just remember what I've said. I'll pick you up from here in a couple of hours. Let's hope that thing lasts that long.' He looked down at the Fireflight Extreme II RTF, the enormous radio-controlled plane that the boys were holding. 'I don't want to see it in pieces.'

'It's alright, Mr Thompson,' said John, 'I've been practising in my garden.'

'Bye, Dad,' said Charlie. 'See you soon. Got a plane to catch.' They both walked off through the Bell Gate and turned left. Once he'd driven off, they quickly doubled back (with Charlie in the lead) and made straight for Granny's yard.

'Why didn't you tell him?' asked John.

'Grown-ups don't understand some things,' said Charlie. He knocked firmly on the door and waited. No reply. He knocked again. Still no reply. He moved to his left and cupped his hands to the window, peering in. No sign of anybody. But he did see what he wanted lying on the table.

Some of her dolls.

He turned round to John. 'There's some right here. I reckon I can reach them.'

'Are you sure she won't mind? When I met her she seemed really nice.'

'She *is* really nice,' said Charlie, 'and *that's* why she won't mind. And it's helping with your project. She loves anything to do with the history of this place.' He gave John the camera. 'Hold this and stand by this window.'

Charlie scrambled onto some flower tubs, leant on John's shoulder to pull himself up on to the narrow sill, and made a grab up for the open smaller window at the top. Once steadied, he reached down inside and flicked back the handle of the side one. Easing it open, he snatched the two nearest figures, handed them over, re-locked the window and jumped down. As Charlie landed, John thought he heard a noise, like a low rumbling, a grumbling throaty sound, from across the yard.

'What was that?' snapped John nervously. 'Near the gate . . .'

'Sorry, didn't hear a thing,' said Charlie. 'Look, just relax. We're only taking photos – it's not like we're kidnapping them or anything. We'll bring them back when we've finished anyway.'

Yenech, held back-to-back against another figure, didn't dare move a muscle. He knew Bybere and Melanak had also come for a winter fitting, but he hadn't seen who (or what) had been seized with him. Was he, she, or it alive?

'This is going to be *so* cool,' said Charlie, helping to carry the plane with his free hand. 'It's not quite like Mistress Masham, but it's a sort of update. The photos should be really good.'

'As long as we don't fly it at top speed,' said John. 'The photos will get blurred at 30 miles an hour.'

Yenech's eyes opened wide. 30 miles? He liked the idea of going that far – but not that quickly.

'How high can it go?' asked Charlie.

'Yes', thought Yenech, 'just how *high* can it go?'

'About 500 feet,' replied John, 'but we shouldn't need to go that high.'

No, thought Yenech, we shouldn't.

Charlie felt the head of one of the dolls wobbling from side to side, and gripped it more tightly to stop it moving.

Once in the field behind Venus, they shooed a few sheep and cows away from the flattest area of grass they could find, and began preparations for the re-enactment of a famous passage from White's book. A short burst confirmed that the 380 electric motor and the rechargeable batteries in the transmitter were in perfect working order, and then the two dolls were folded into the seats behind one another, the male in combats in the front. Charlie thought it was a really neat idea to have this one's arms stuck up, as if it was in the front seat of a roller-coaster. Yenech kept his fixed grin.

'Oh no,' said John, 'I knew we'd forgotten something. Seatbelts.' At that very moment the right arm of the soldier doll swung down inside the cockpit. Charlie noticed it drop and twisted it back up again. 'Yeh, I suppose you're right. Granny won't be happy if one of them falls out.' Yenech's fixed grin was about to snap.

'I know,' continued Charlie. 'Laces, from our trainers.' They were duly pulled out and tied round the two little figures, which made at least one of them much happier – until he heard the next comment from John.

'I don't know how the extra weight will affect it. It *should* take-off, but anything could happen after that.'

'There's only one way to find out,' replied Charlie enthusiastically. 'Ready? Chocks away!'

John pressed a button, the electric motor leapt into life, and Yenech prepared himself to leap into the next life. The propeller hurtled round, throwing a blast of cold air full in the face of the laced-up tiny soldier with erect arms, a tight smile and an assumed short life-expectancy. He also had his eyes shut, which meant that he only *felt* the bouncing of the aircraft as it hit bumps and hollows along the runway – and he felt them all – before it was replaced by the smooth sensation of flying.

This gave a moment of relief until he opened his eyes and found himself about to have a close encounter with the face of a startled black-and-white cow.

'Quick!' shouted Charlie. 'Mind that cow!'

'Don't worry,' said John, 'I've flown this loads of times.' Which was true, but never when it had two pilots inside. The plane reacted more sluggishly, and just cleared the top of the animal's head, the fuselage passing between its ears.

Yenech missed seeing it but smelt everything.

'Sorry,' said John, 'I hadn't allowed for the passengers. I'll fly it round in circles and we'll get some pictures.'

The next five minutes proved to be the best part of the flight. Yenech's arms were beginning to ache slightly, but otherwise the experience was enjoyable, even exhilarating. He also had a bird's-eye view of the gardens, and reckoned that he never need get lost again. The experience was only spoiled by Charlie saying, 'Can I have a go?' That question and its consequences turned Yenech's world upside-down, and his stomach inside-out.

Luckily there was no way that his screams could be heard 300 feet below as the hugely expensive and impressive Fireflight Extreme II went into a vertical climb. But they were audible to the person seated behind – or more strictly, *below* – him. 'Keep calm, soldier,' came the voice – a female voice. 'If you want to stay alive, do *exactly* what I say. First . . .' Her words were drowned by a rush of wind and another lengthy scream as the plane reached the apex of its climb, briefly hung in the air, and then started an inexorable vertical dive, twisting round as it did so.

'Hold on,' came the voice again, which he now recognized as Melanak, 'I'm just undoing your laces.'

'Nooooo!' shouted Yenech, 'Yeaaargghhhh!' as the plane fiercely pulled out of its high-speed corkscrew plummet and skimmed across the surface of Copper Bottom Lake, spray catching him in the face.

'We've only got one chance,' yelled Melanak. 'It's the batteries. They'll run out soon. The extra weight.'

Charlie was putting the aircraft through its paces. He executed a couple of perfect loops, inside and out, and then a rather tricky manoeuvre that surprised him (and others). 'What was that?' he asked John. 'A half-barrel roll,' came the reply.

Yenech leant over the side and made a violent noise. 'What was that?' asked Melanak. 'Half a breakfast roll,' came the reply.

At the summit of the next climb, Yenech found that he was totally free of the straps; Melanak had done her stuff. He gratefully allowed his arms to swing down and clasp hold of the sides. As they circled high above Venus and the Eleven-Acre Lake, he heard the next command. 'That wire by your right foot, pull it hard, now!'

Yenech did as he was told. It didn't seem to make any difference.

'Something's happened,' said Charlie, handing back the transmitter to John.

'That's weird,' said John. 'I've lost the signal. It's flying itself.'

Which it wasn't. Melanak had found the wires for the elevators, and Yenech was pulling hard on the rudder lever as instructed. He was enjoying being told where to go, and, as he reflected later, 'You can't get lost in the sky, it's just open space . . .'

'We can't have much more time,' shouted Melanak above the noise of the engine, 'any minute now . . .' and suddenly her words became louder as they no longer competed with the engine – because it had stopped.

'Yenech, we're now in a *glider*. Pull left, hard, and make for the corner down there by the boat-hut – harder! *Pull!*'

Yenech duly pulled, and the craft began to swoop down towards the water, like some sort of angular swan. 'When I say so, lean over as far as you can on the right.' Yenech nodded.

'We've lost it,' muttered John grimly. 'It's heading straight for the hut. And the dolls are coming loose.'

'Sorry,' said Charlie. 'My fault. I'll explain to Granny if they get broken.'

'Now!' screamed Melanak, and their combined efforts to destabilise the aeroplane succeeded spectacularly as it flipped over and began flying upside-down.

'Hang on!' shouted Melanak.

'I will, don't worry!' shouted Yenech in reply.

'Any second now . . .' said John. 'I can't watch.'

'Any second now . . .' said Melanak. 'Watch . . . now! Jump!'

One would think that any averagely sane person, occupying a fairly safe seat in an aircraft, would not heed that instruction, but Yenech had years of army training behind him, and his instincts left him no alternative. He found himself obeying the order, and also found himself briefly falling, and then landing on some netting – which then catapulted him back into the air when another body landed nearby.

Just prior to hearing his own 'splash' as he hit the water, he heard a 'whump' as a Fireflight Extreme II made an unscheduled stop against a boat-hut. His next sensation was his collar being grasped by a pair of firm but gentle hands, and being pulled out of the lake towards the netting of the duck decoy.

It took a few minutes for the boys in trainers (without laces) to flip-flop over to the crash-site and inspect the damage. The plane was a write-off, nor could they find their laces anywhere, but they were surprised and relieved to find Granny's two dolls caught up in the netting, although one was half-in the water.

'This one's a bit wet,' said Charlie, 'but the other one's fine.'

'Not just fine,' thought Yenech, 'she's perfect. Absolutely perfect.'

The Lord of the Manor of Chackmore was inspecting his new estate and centre of operations with one of his trusted men, who was struggling with his walking-stick to keep up with his boss. Near the end of the main driveway, past the new huts and installations, a scrawny youth suddenly appeared at the wrought-iron gates, thrusting his hand through and waving an envelope. Biddle scowled at such rudeness, but motioned to his assistant to deal with him.

On his return, he ripped open the letter, recognising the scrawl immediately.

> *Dear Sir,*
> *You will be glad to know that I made excellent contact with two of the people yesterday. I was keeping an eye on your son as usual, and he put two figures into a model aeroplane he was flying with Charlie Thompson.*

Biddle became impatient. Why couldn't Newbold get straight to the point? He read on.

> *The boys crashed it into the boathouse, near where I was hiding, but the two Lilliputians fell out just beforehand. I was close enough to recognise that they were a male and a female; indeed the male was the one that I captured a few weeks ago.*

'Incompetent fool,' thought Biddle.

> *I'm afraid to say that your son displayed no awareness that these two were alive, treating them just as dolls. He undoubtedly lacks the sight. I was not able to capture these two Lilliputians because the two boys ran over very quickly and got there ahead of me.*
> *Yours,*
> *Julius Newbold*

Biddle stood there re-reading the letter. He was angry. Angry at his son's inability, doubtless inherited from his father. Angry that a common failure like Newbold should nevertheless possess such a gift, a gift that by rights belonged to the Biddle line. And angry that the fool was making so little progress. He took out a pen, and wrote forcefully in large capitals on the reverse.

NO MORE EXCUSES
NO MORE LETTERS
NO MORE CHANCES

'Return to sender,' he remarked gruffly, holding out the paper. The recipient hobbled to the gates and the waiting youth.

The Lord of the Manor turned swiftly on his heels and marched towards the house and his study. There would be no more letters from Newbold, but he himself now had a few to write.

11 : The Decoy

As soon as Jamie walked in the front door that evening, he heard his father in the sitting room. He was using his sternest voice.

'I gave you *clear* instructions, Charlie,' he said angrily, speaking in clipped tones. 'That plane was *not* a toy. It was *not* for fooling around with. It was a *special* machine. It cost a *lot* of money.'

From the hallway, Jamie caught the muffled apology. 'This,' he thought, 'is a *very* promising scenario.' Dropping his bag on the stairs, he quietly walked in. Mr Thompson, face set firm, stood in front of Charlie, who was looking suitably abashed and guilty. Mrs Thompson was seated on the sofa, hands in her lap, her expression sad and resigned.

'What's happened?' Jamie asked. (He really wanted to say, 'What's he done *now*?' but sensibly thought better of it.)

Charlie glared at him. 'None of your. . . .'

'That's enough, young man,' said his father. 'Jamie needs to know. It might be awkward for him.' He composed himself. 'Charlie went off with John Biddle to fly his remote-controlled aircraft. Charlie got stupid, and crashed it into the boathouse on the Eleven-Acre.'

Jamie paused before replying. On the one hand, it was always satisfying to see Charlie put in his place, but on the other he was pleased that things had turned out badly for John Biddle. So, unde-cided whether to condemn or congratulate his brother, he chose a rather bored, 'Oh, right.'

Mr Thompson was surprised by his older son's evident lack of interest, but resumed his complaint against the younger one. 'And have you apologised to Granny yet?'

Jamie was suddenly interested. 'Why should he apologise to Granny?'

'Because he broke into the cottage, stole a couple of her dolls, tied them into the plane, and could have damaged them beyond repair.'

Jamie sat down. This was much more serious.

'Which ones?' he asked, hoping he sounded casual.

He didn't. The others all turned towards him in unison, puzzled at his question. A moment of silence, then Jamie repeated himself, this time with an obvious urgency. '*Which* ones?'

Mr Thompson looked down at Charlie. 'Can you remember?'

'Not really – why does it matter anyway?'

'Some of them really mean a lot to her,' said Jamie. 'Did you actually *break* any?'

Mrs Thompson answered. 'Jamie, they're fine. They fell out of the aircraft and landed on the new duck decoy. One fell in the water, but I expect Granny's tidied them up by now.'

'So *which* ones were they?'

'For goodness' sake,' groaned Charlie, 'this is ridiculous!' Then he caught the irritated look on his father's face. 'Alright then, I think one was a man in combats and the other was a girl. I can't remember what she was wearing.'

'Usual male problem, Charlie,' said Mrs Thompson under her breath.

Jamie's mind was in rather a whirl. He knew that Yenech had intended to visit Granny earlier, so he may well have just 'enjoyed' the most exciting trip of his life, but who was the female? Jamie also realised that, in spite of this alarming news, there was one reassuring aspect – Charlie knew nothing about the secret life of the dolls.

Charlie himself now decided it was time to divert attention away from his own misdemeanours, and towards his brother and his romances. This was the perfect opportunity and he went for it. 'This doll thing. It's your *girlfriend*, isn't it?'

'*What*?' said Jamie.

'What?' said Dad.

'*Really*?' said Mum. 'Who is she? Since when? Where does she live?'

Charlie folded his arms smugly. 'Go on, Jamie, tell them.' No response; his brother was speechless. 'Well, if *you* won't, *I* will.' He happily addressed his parents. 'It all started a while ago, she's called Maria, she lives around here somewhere, and she really likes old poetry and flowers and stuff like that, and that's why Jamie has got interested, *and* she's lending him books about Malplaquet, and John Biddle used to be her special friend, but *he* won't admit it either, and . . .'

His father's raised hand stopped him. 'Anything to say, Jamie?'

'Lots,' he replied. 'Do you want to know the truth?'

'Yes, please,' said Mum eagerly, on the edge of her seat. 'Everything.'

'Charlie found out some time ago. I *have* been seeing someone, and she lives quite close, and she does like gardens and poetry. She lent me a book as well, and her name is Maria, and she's lovely.' The end of the sentence was marked by a soft sigh of 'Aah,' by his mum. Charlie felt very satisfied with himself and his detective work. Unfortunately for him, Jamie hadn't finished his confession.

'And she's got a nickname.'

'Which is?' asked Mum, keen for any additional information.

'Granny,' said Jamie. 'Aka Maria. There *is* no girlfriend.'

Mrs Thompson, as if punctured, flopped back into her chair.

Mr Thompson spoke up. 'Charlie, you're an utter berk. Anything else to add to your performance this morning?'

Charlie shook his head, knowing he'd made a complete fool of himself. There was only one way to retrieve the situation. As the two boys left the room and made their way upstairs, he calmly said to his older brother, 'I think my little plan worked very well.'

'Little plan?' queried Jamie.

'To distract the enemy. Create a diversion and beat a retreat. Standard military practice.'

'Not bad,' acknowledged Jamie, 'very cunning. Almost as cunning as my diversion about Granny.' He sauntered on and shut his bedroom door.

Charlie was left outside, thinking hard. He knocked on the door politely. 'Jamie?' No reply. 'Jamie, come on, you can tell me, I'm your brother. I won't tell anybody, honest. *Jamie* . . . ?'

Julius Newbold had been panicking for a few days. Having his letter returned from Jedekiah Biddle with its threatening footnote had been a real shock. He had no idea that his employer was in such a hurry, and he really thought he'd been doing his best. After all, he argued to himself, he'd spent months hiding in little more than a sodden ditch, had actually captured some of the Lilliputians (before they got lucky and escaped), had been faithfully tracking the son, *and* had confirmed that the boy – just like his father – could not see the tiny people. Furthermore, he had even forged old documents to indicate the previous existence of a duck decoy at Malplaquet, in the hope of using it as a trap – but, just his luck, it had recently saved the lives of two of the little blighters.

For all these reasons – despite Biddle's words in the letter – Julius thought that he still had one more chance. But he also knew that it would be his last.

It was time to put the decoy into action, and he would need some help from unusual quarters.

'Goodness me, Vicky,' said Granny, her breath forming billows of faint moisture over the newcomer, 'what on earth are you doing here at *this* time of the day? I've not even had my breakfast yet.' A low and watery sun was struggling to make any impact on the chilly and damp air of the November morning.

'Sorry,' panted Vicky, 'but one of the volunteers phoned me half an hour ago. They're doing a practice run on the new decoy, and they need another pair of hands.' She paused to take a deep breath. 'I thought I'd better come and keep an eye on things. I don't know why it has to be done so early."

'You're right,' agreed Granny. 'Leave it to me – I'll make sure you're not on your own. But are you sure you're warm enough? What about a scarf and gloves?'

'No, I'm okay, this fleece is fine. Got to go – I'm meeting them just past Venus.' She turned and dashed off, giving Florence the lion a cautious glance and a slight berth.

Granny quickly shut the door to keep the heat in, and looked around at Nigriff. He was standing spread-eagled against a mug of Hot Chocolate, enjoying the warmth of the unorthodox but effective radiator. 'Squirrels?' she asked.

'Squirrels it is, Madam' came the reply.

'And the TQS?' she added.

'I believe you mean the *new* TQS,' he said. 'Although I may not be *far* away – this hot drink has really invigorated me this morning.'

Vicky found Ralph at the far end of the Lake, and decided that Granny would approve of his garb: scarf and gloves, heavy-duty Wellingtons, waterproof trousers, and a quilted green waistcoat under his well-worn waxed brown jacket. A grunt of welcome was followed by an order to 'stay right here, miss,' on the bank, about fifty yards in front of the decoy. Then he shuffled off, a sackcloth bag slung over one shoulder.

She began to tremble slightly, partly from the chill, which was even more invasive down by the water, but also from nerves. Something was troubling her. As Ralph rounded the final corner, Vicky took in a few details of the decoy.

It was a narrow inlet of water, curving away from the end of the lake, covered by a tunnel of netting. This was supported by metal hoops which gradually reduced in size until, at the far end, it was simply a net bag, which the decoyman would remove with the trapped duck inside – or what ever else had been caught in it.

Vicky shivered again. At least she didn't have to be worried about any Lilliputians; it was surely too cold for them to be about.

Just outside the tunnel along one bank ran a series of reed fences. They were two metres high, with gaps between them. The Trust's expert adviser had explained their purpose. A 'decoyman' would hide behind the first fence, awaiting the ducks. Once some had come close, he would order his dog (ideally a Dutch breed called a *Kooikerhondje*) to run past the first screen and through the gap. The ducks, naturally curious of other animals, would enter the tunnel. The dog would reappear further on down . . . the unsuspecting ducks would follow . . . and so on, until they were far into the pipe. The decoyman would then appear from behind, and shoo the ducks towards the net bag, where their journey finished (until they much later re-appeared on a smart dining plate).

Vicky was just wondering where the dog was – and the ducks as well – when she saw Ralph's helper on the other bank by the boathouse. He waved (which Vicky thought was very friendly), and held up a length of rope with its end in the water. Vicky waved back, and jumped up and down, trying to keep warm.

She suddenly noticed a series of light splashes at the decoy's entrance, where Ralph was scattering pellets. The bait dropped, he hid behind the first fence.

However, there was still no sign of a dog, Dutch or any other nationality.

She wondered what was going to happen.

'I wonder what's going to happen,' panted Hyroc, jogging behind the other three.

'No idea,' said Yenech out in front. 'The instructions weren't that clear. We're the back-up for Miss Vicky at the duck trap.' He readjusted the long cloth bag that each carried on their backs. On a human, it might suggest a long gun or a thick fishing rod. On a Lilliputian, it could be anything, from a bundle of pencils to a fat cigar.

In spite of their burdens, they progressed well along the shredded bark path on the north side of the lake. Unfortunately, that uneven and frosty ground did sometimes cause one of the team to stumble and sprawl headlong, the heavy pack almost pinning the person down. Yenech was acting as a true leader, being very considerate about his team's welfare, especially that of the new recruit – who was grateful for Yenech's helping hand. 'Thanks – I do appreciate it,' was the comment after the latest fall.

'My pleasure,' was his response, leaning over the prone figure. 'I'm sorry your first mission is so tough.'

'Don't worry,' came the silky reply, 'I *prefer* things that are tough.'

Yenech needed no encouragement. 'Come on, men!' he shouted. 'Follow me!'

Without knowing exactly why, Vicky was becoming increasingly apprehensive. A few ducks had now arrived, and were happily en-joying breakfast near the tunnel, pecking and dipping and snaffling. Despite their splashes, she also thought she heard across the lake the GT's gentle hum.

At that moment her partner by the boat-hut lifted his rope higher, a line moved across the water, and, looking down, Vicky spotted her rope sliding away below a bush. She bent down, pulled it tight, and out of the lake appeared a dripping net. The instructions were yelled across to her. 'Walk to the decoy!' She duly obliged, dragging her side forwards as the man stayed where he was.

She had no idea where Ralph had got to.

But, way down the tunnel, she did see some fish that had swum in there for safety, their heads breaking the surface.

Except that they weren't the heads of fish.

They were human arms. *Tiny* human arms, splashing over and over as their owners fled the encroaching net.

Vicky suddenly remembered. It had to be Chamklab and his training-partner Traclev, two Cascadians, fanatical athletes, who swam and ran in all weathers.

Alarmed, she looked across and watched the man drag his end of the net very close to the pipe's entrance. Two quick-witted ducks cleared the low net in a frenzy of flapping and thus escaped, but the greedier ones were nonchalantly following the trail of food. And the two tiny figures were not far behind.

Vicky glanced across the Eleven-Acre, and saw the GT making its usual spectacularly slow progress; it would be ages before it arrived. She made a rapid decision. Throwing her rope into the water, the splash causing a commotion amongst the ducks, she ran swiftly towards the boathouse island past the end of the decoy.

There was no sign of Ralph – nor any tiny figures in the water.

Slithering her way across the concrete causeway with its rusted handrails, she squelched round to the hut, where she came face to face with the volunteer. He still had his rope, but now, as he sat hunched up, it was tightly wrapped and knotted around his hands and knees.

Before him was a semicircle of four tiny figures – three male, one female – each brandishing a human dinner-fork, and jabbing it towards the miserable captive in a threatening manner. He wasn't happy.

'Everything under control here, Miss Vicky,' said Yenech. 'You need to find the other human. If this one moves, we'll soon make a meal of him.'

'Okay,' said Vicky, shocked at the turn of events. She ran to the end of the island, and came to a stop. Ralph was bending over Traclev and Chamklab, pulling a towel out of his bag, and wrapping it round each of them, as if bundling them up.

He looked up at her and smiled. 'They're safe now, Miss Vicky, everything's fine.'

The two Cascadians gave her a smile and a thumbs-up. It was difficult to find the words to say; she had clearly misjudged Ralph.

He spoke first. 'How's our prisoner back there? Not exactly saved by the cavalry, more like savaged by the cutlery!'

'But I thought . . . and *you* can see them . . .'

'Indeed, Miss Vicky, and have done for many years. And so can Julius.'

'Who?' said Vicky.

'Breakfast,' indicated Ralph, nodding in his direction. He finished drying the swimmers. 'Time for a run, chaps,' he said. 'Warm yourselves up.' They murmured their gratitude, waved happily, and sprinted off on the next phase of their training.

Ralph packed the towel away in his bag, and laughed to himself as a few ducks waddled happily through the open end of the decoy. '*They* won't be frightened of this place again,' he chuckled, 'unlike our tasty friend. Come on, let's send him on his way, and I need a chat with Miss Maria. I've been looking forward to this for years, so I suppose I can wait another half hour for her buggy . . . .'

'Does *anybody* know why we're here?' asked Brian Dedd, Head of Information, looking at the blank faces of the National Trust managers round the table.

His question was met only by a slight echo in the gracious but cold room of the Queen's Temple, with its heart-warming views and feet-freezing temperature. Only two weeks to go until Christmas, when sensible people were panicking over their shopping lists or anxiously surfing the internet for cheap flights to warmer climes, and the Director-General had called an urgent meeting at Malplaquet of her national and regional key players. All the 'great and the good' were there, as well as several of the 'mediocre and inoffensive' and two of the 'just plain nasty.' The only person who was missing was Len Scaype, the Property Manager of Malplaquet.

'At least we've got decent biscuits,' said Gary Baldiss, Head of

Catering, munching on his third.

'Our new line,' said Bill Board, the Marketing Manager, 'locally and organically made, using traditional ancient ingredients, in a traditional ancient manner by our traditional . . . er . . . by our most valued helpers.'

'We give them to visiting children,' remarked a flushed Toyah Letts-Close, the Visitor Services Manager.

'What? For free?' added Sonia Bille, the Regional Financial Controller.

'I hope you've done a Risk Assessment,' added the national Legal Adviser, Lou Poles.

'Thank you all for coming,' interrupted a crisp and refined voice by the pair of glass doors. The sharp words startled them. Their understandable focus on pre-agenda Item One had diverted them from the arrival of the Director-General herself, an awesome incarnation of efficiency and professionalism.

At her side stood a man exuding equal confidence and power, the collar of his dark overcoat turned up against the chill air. His thin smile, lacking any warmth, significantly added to the bleak atmosphere of the December day.

The pair strode across the room together, two sets of expensive heels striking the parquet floor. 'I appreciate the time it has taken you all to get here, especially on a Sunday afternoon.' She took her seat at the head of the table, motioning to her guest to sit on her left. The Head of Catering duly poured two cups of coffee, looking in vain for any biscuits. 'I am confident that by the end of this meeting, you will be as excited as I am about the Trust's work at Malplaquet.' She sipped at her coffee. Aware of nothing to nibble, her long experience at high-powered sessions paid off, as she discreetly spotted excessive crumbs on the plate of the Director of Expansion (despite his carefully placed sleeve). She made a mental note to herself. 'But forgive me; let me introduce the owner of Chackmore Manor, Mr Jedekiah Biddle.' Polite applause followed, with most wondering why a local newcomer was present.

They didn't have to wait long.

'I am delighted to announce,' she continued, 'that as of this moment Mr. Biddle is the *new* Property Manager of Malplaquet.' She registered their shock, and answered the question that she knew was on everybody's mind. 'Len, who has been such a loyal servant of the Trust, has recently been wanting to step back from his responsibility. We are fortunate that his, er . . . *unrest* coincided neatly with Mr. Biddle's arrival.'

There was still an awkward silence in the room. Nobody could believe what she was saying about Len. He had always loved the place and his job.

The Director-General continued. 'I must at the very start highlight Mr. Biddle's commitment to, and interest in, Malplaquet. Following a tip-off, I can reveal that the substantial donation that began our campaign here came from none other than Jedekiah himself.' He tried to appear suitably humble, and there were even a couple of murmurs of appreciation. The good lady completed her introduction. 'And now, Mr. Biddle, we would be thrilled to hear of your *extraordinary* plans for our gardens.'

He rose imperiously to his feet, and, at the conclusion of his impressive forty-minute speech, no-one was in any doubt that he was fully intent on transforming Malplaquet. 'I want to make it come *alive*!' were his closing words of triumph, as he resumed his seat to steady and appreciative applause. Dear old Len was already history. The buzz of excited comments round the table ranged from 'really bring in the crowds,' and 'fantastic ideas,' to 'wake the place up a bit,' and 'should take the biscuit.'

That last one, from the Director of Expansion, unfortunately came over loud and clear in a sudden lull in the conversation. His boss soon dismissed the rest of the troops, said a fond and grateful farewell to her new appointment, and led the Director to one corner for a quiet word.

He knew it was crunch time.

12 : Goodwill to all Men

'Have you finished your Christmas shopping yet, Jamie?' asked Granny, as she raked over the fire and put another log on top of the glowing coals.

'Not yet, but I found a book for Charlie this morning. He's needed it for ages.'

'Oh, that is kind. He'll be so pleased. What's it called?'

'*Increase Your Brain Power,*' said Jamie. 'It's our last hope.'

'Hmm,' said Granny. 'Sounds more like trouble.'

'On the contrary, Madam,' added Nigriff, 'it sounds perfect. And I'm sure that Jamie will want to read it afterwards.'

'Is that meant to be funny?' Jamie asked, actually half-hoping that it was. Nigriff had been developing a wry sense of humour in recent weeks.

'Of course not, sir,' he replied. 'I never joke about matters of the intellect. They are far too serious.'

Jamie didn't know what to make of that comment. 'Anyway, Granny,' he said, 'you were going to tell me all about Ralph.'

She smiled across at him. 'It's amazing,' she said. 'After all these years. Never thought I'd see the dear chap again.'

'So was he just one of your gardeners?'

'Not just *one* – the best. Only a young fellow when he started, but you could see from the word go that he loved the place. You would have thought he had green blood, not just green fingers.'

Nigriff was shocked. 'I have had only a brief acquaintance with him, Madam, but I can assure you that his digits are not . . .'

'It's a *saying*, Nigriff,' interrupted Jamie. 'Someone with 'green fingers' is a natural gardener. You need to read more; Charlie can lend you a good book after Christmas.'

'Is that meant to be funny, Master Jamie?'

'Of course not, Nigriff. I never joke about matters of the intellect.'

'You two are getting worse,' sighed Granny. 'Now, where was I? Oh yes, Ralph, he used to work for me – in fact, come to think of it, he built some of the Model City, the houses mainly.'

'Which is where he first saw the Lilliputians, I suppose,' said Jamie.

'Probably,' agreed Granny, 'but he certainly knew about them when I sold up. Then he got a job not far away – Waddesdon, he says – so he could keep half an eye on them. And, come to think of it, perhaps on me as well . . . I wonder . . .'

'You have been fortunate in your friends,' said Nigriff.

'Unlike J Newbold,' added Jamie. 'How did he join up with Biddle?'

'Ralph's been asking round, it's all very murky,' said Granny. 'Money problems. Ralph also said he spotted Newbold in the gardens earlier this year, snooping round the temples and acting as if he could see the Lilliputians. So Ralph hung around here a lot as well; he was actually nearby when Newbold got tipped into the lake. More cake anyone?'

Jamie happily tucked into a thick wedge of the chocolate sponge, and Nigriff was given some decent-sized crumbs and the Smartie off the top. Granny resumed her story. 'But Ralph knew that Julius couldn't give up whilst Biddle was still threatening him, so when Julius joined the Volunteers, Ralph did as well.'

'Didn't Vicky say that Newbold looked totally different, plastic surgery and all that? She'd no idea it was him – he'd changed so much. She feels bad that she didn't spot him.'

'There are two features, Master Jamie, that even extensive nipping and tucking and other reconstructing cannot hide – one's eyes and one's gait.'

'What's a gate got to do with it?'

'Gait with an 'i' in it,' said Nigriff.

'A gate with an eye in it?' asked Jamie. 'What's that about?'

Granny untangled the linguistic confusion, and told Jamie she'd buy him a good book for Christmas, called *Increase Your Word Power*. And yes, that was a joke. Sort of.

'So, with Newbold out of the way, all's well that ends well,' concluded Jamie. 'Which is Shakespeare – see, I do read a lot. Can you match that, Nigriff?'

'Measure for measure,' came the reply, 'and as you like it, let us hope that this comedy of errors was much ado about nothing . . . and that our forthcoming winter's tale will not be a tempest.'

'I should give up, Jamie,' prompted Granny. 'You can't do much with Henry IV Part 1. And Biddle can't do much with Newbold. Ralph told him that if he ever saw *any* of his faces here in the grounds again, his guilty secrets would be out. No, dear Julius is dead in the water.' Nigriff raised an eyebrow at this last comment.

'Just another saying, Nigriff,' explained Jamie. 'And with any luck, Biddle's panicking. He's lost his eyes and ears in the grounds ('another saying,' said Granny this time), and everyone in the village hates him. No-one goes near the Manor anymore – he's really spoilt the place.'

'I fear you may be underestimating him, sir,' said Nigriff sombrely. 'His local reputation is irrelevant. His focus of attention is the gardens themselves.'

'Sure,' said Jamie, 'but what can he do there? No-one knows him. And we couldn't find anything else in the prophecy still to do – so we *must* have almost won.'

'If that is true, sir – and I do hope that you are right – then the Forces of Restoration have proven themselves to be most powerful. My fear is that we have not yet seen anything like the full extent of the Forces of Destruction.'

Granny sighed. 'Nigriff, this is a time of year when we *celebrate*, not worry about vaguely possible problems.' She began to clear the plates away. 'How about a *Merry* Christmas?'

'And a *Happy* New Year?' asked Jamie.

'Of course,' replied Nigriff. 'I do beg your pardon. I hope that we can all look forward to an excellent period ahead – especially, I might add, Yenech.'

'Why Yenech?' said Jamie.

'TQS are having difficulty in replacing Yours Truly. Yenech is spending *considerable* time and energy personally training a young lady. Judging by their long walks, her fitness levels are not yet adequate.'

'I'm sure Yenech knows what he's doing,' said Granny. 'He told me she has real potential.'

The feeble street-lights in Chackmore High Street didn't show the puddle in front of Jamie until it was too late.

'Urgh, yuk!' he exclaimed, jumping to one side. 'I *said* we needed a torch.'

'For goodness' sake, stop moaning,' said Dad. 'You've been at it all day. And don't get in Granny's way. Hold her arm.'

'And it is Christmas Eve,' said Mum.

'*Exactly*,' said Jamie. 'The time when we stay home and play board games. It's tradition.'

'Well, it's nice to do something different for a change,' replied Dad.

'And you just want to win,' said Charlie. 'Which you wouldn't have done.'

'*Would* have,' said Jamie, 'as usual. And it would be better than going to the Manor and eating dry mince pies and flaky sausage-rolls.'

'Lady Harrison-Smythe always did her best,' chided Mum. 'It's the thought that counts.'

'In that case, I'll just think about them and not eat them,' replied Jamie.

'I wouldn't be worried about dodgy food,' said his father. 'The number of catering vans and lorries going past this week has been amazing. And what's that smell? Vanilla? Caramel?'

The light, as well as the sweet aroma, was becoming stronger as they walked under the shadow of the high brick wall surrounding the Manor. The sounds of excited chatter and the yells of children also broke through the gloom, as did the shouting of stallholders and the strains of piped music, just like a fairground.

'Come on, Jamie,' whispered Granny. 'Cheer up. It's a chance to joint the case anyway.'

'Case the joint,' corrected Jamie.

'We'll do that as well,' said Granny. 'If there's time.'

They stood by the wrought-iron gates, which all week had been boarded over to stop prying eyes and heighten curiosity. Mr. Thompson yanked the chain of the bell hanging on the nearest pillar. On its first ring, the gates swung back, each pulled by a life-size furry snowman, the figures bending forward in perfect unison and welcoming them with a wide sweep of a thick white arm. The family looked down the drive. It was difficult to take in the whole magical scene at once.

It was the light that struck them first, bursting on their eyes and making them squint after the semi-darkness of the village lanes. On either side of the avenue, powerful floodlights were reflecting off swirls of snowflakes pumped from massive tubes, and shining through dazzling ice-sculptures. The nearest ones were a polar bear, a couple skating arm-in-arm, a group of penguins, and an enormous replica of Malplaquet's statue of George I on horseback. Almost in a daze and looking from side to side, the family slowly walked past merry-go-rounds, candy-floss stalls, juggling entertainers on stilts, and chestnuts being roasted on red-hot braziers and popped into paper cones. In the distance were fire-eaters, clowns on unicycles, more snowmen, and gnomes by barbecues serving up sizzling bacon and onions and sausages. The smell of toffee and popcorn drifting in the cool misty air was mouth-watering.

'Wow!' approved Charlie. 'This is *awesome*.'

'My word,' said Mum. 'I've never seen anything like it.'

'Right, Jamie,' said Dad. 'Let's find that dry mince pie you remembered.'

'This is *so* tacky,' said Jamie. 'This isn't Christmas. It's a con. He just wants people to like him, and then . . .'

'Leave him to me,' said Granny to his parents, shepherding him gently to one side. 'You go off and enjoy yourselves.' Jamie twisted out of reach, watching his parents wander off arm-in-arm, whilst Charlie dashed over to John Biddle who was standing by a ramp with his new skateboard and waving at him. 'That John really *is* such a nice boy,' murmured Granny with approval.

Jamie wasn't convinced, and scowled in his direction, but it was the older Biddle he was more bothered about. 'Granny, can't you see what's happening? We've *got* to stop him.'

'Of course I can, but we can't stop this, and certainly not by moaning about it. All we can do tonight is try to see what he's up to.'

Jamie looked around, very frustrated. He didn't like the idea of the local people being deceived; Biddle was a villain, and they ought to know the truth as soon as possible. 'Alright,' he said reluctantly, 'but it still bothers me.'

'Me too,' said Granny, 'so let's get to work.'

There was no denying the fact that Biddle had laid on the most fantastic Christmas celebration, with something for all tastes and ages. An artificial skating-rink had been built, with equipment and tuition provided (Jamie was dismayed and embarrassed to see his parents trying it out, clinging to each other like a pair of giggly adolescents). Elves were doling out generous quantities of mulled wine, or fluorescent cocktails in frosted glasses. Families were dressing-up in Victorian clothes to have faded brown photos taken. Arcade games were lined up in one marquee, all for free, with the most popular one allowing you to test your sleigh-driving skills. Soaring from roof-top to roof-top, you had to avoid factory chimneys and tall pylons, hold your course in freak side-winds and thick fog, ignore predatory sea-gulls, and encourage your tiring reindeer by flapping the reins more and more vigorously. Granny registered the night's High Score when she landed the sleigh on top of a speedboat zig-zagging under Tower Bridge.

'Lost none of the old skills,' she said stepping down, sucking on a peppermint.

'Old skills?' thought Jamie. 'When has she done *that* before?'

On the main forecourt of the Manor stood the perfect cone of a wonderful Christmas tree, covered in a dangling mass of celebratory items that would satisfy people of any belief or none. The two of them wandered past, pushed their way into the entrance-hall, and cast their eyes around. Granny spotted the old portrait first.

'Captain Biddle, I presume,' she said. 'Funny, he doesn't look that evil.'

'Who doesn't?' said a hard voice from behind. She turned and met the unsmiling stare of a man wearing an eighteenth-century frock coat, a wide-brimmed hat, and a white Venetian mask framing his eyes and the top half of his face. He was also grasping a walking-stick.

'That famous sea-captain,' she said, completely unruffled. 'Just something I thought I'd heard. Probably got it wrong. Anyway, can't stop, nice to meet you.' A hand on Jamie's shoulder and they were off down the nearest corridor.

'Close,' said Jamie.

'Quite,' said Granny.

They checked out all the available entertainments. In the kitchen was a highly imaginative cookery demonstration entitled, '101 Uses for a Dead Turkey.' The sitting room was full of people playing traditional parlour-games – which had been corrected and up-dated to Hunt the Trainer, Emailer's Knock, Musical Bean-bags, and Simone Suggests. A 'Carolathon' round the piano was proving popular in the Lesser Drawing-room, and the basement cinema was showing the new Bollywood Christmas disaster epic, about the raging monsoon that nearly wrecked a young couple's wedding – 'Looks like Reindeer.' All these were obviously enticing, but *the* place to be was inevitably the dining room.

Its ancient panelling was festooned in a heady riot of leafy garlands and wreaths, glossy holly, shimmering lights and candles. The long central table, draped in a white star-spattered cloth, was bearing the weight of the rich and festive food. Granny was almost overcome as she read out the decorative labels.

'Toasts with Venison pate, Tortilla Wraps of Parma Ham and Ricotta with Sage, Coconut and Saffron Prawns, Spicy Chicken Wings, Sole Goujons, and just look at those wonderful Parmesan Button Mushrooms!' Jamie didn't respond. It sounded tasty enough, but he really wanted to ignore it all if he could. That was the last thought in Granny's mind as she continued on her grand tour of the table.

'Honey and Mustard Chipolatas, Smoked Salmon and Cream Cheese Roules, Turkey Caesar Wraps, Baby Yorkshire Puddings, Asparagus Spears wrapped in the Finest Serrano Ham, Crostini with Pate de Foie Gras and Truffles . . .'

Jamie was now weakening. He had no idea what they might taste like, but they all sounded irresistibly delicious. It was the sweets that finally tipped him over the edge: Baby Christmas Puddings, Chocolate Dipped Fruits, Fresh Cream Pastries, Moist Orange and Almond Cake, and the simply irresistible Chocolate Fudge Cake – with lashings of Brandy Butter.

'I suppose I *could* try a mince pie,' Jamie said, showing remarkable self-discipline and nonchalantly picking up the nearest creation. It was unbelievably gorgeous: deliciously warm, soft and full of tender fruit. It actually melted inside his mouth, the spices gently tickling his throat. It had clearly never known the loving touch of Lady Harrison-Smythe.

He quickly grabbed another, and was about to fill a large empty plate when a bell rang not far away. There was a collective moan of disappointment, and then the guests began to file out. Jamie and Granny shuffled along the corridor with them, the old lady juggling several items from the finger buffet.

Back in the Hall, she spotted the Georgian man again, guarding a door that was slightly ajar, and occasionally craning his neck through the gap.

'I bet *that* room's worth seeing,' whispered Granny. 'Distract him.'

'What!?' gasped Jamie, taken aback.

'Anything you like,' said Granny. 'I just need a minute.'

Jamie thought for a moment, and casually walked over, before suddenly bending forward and clutching his stomach. He produced a loud retching sound – '*Urrgggh!*' – and yelled, 'I'm going to throw up!'

It worked brilliantly; the guard was caught by surprise. He looked around for help, found none, and quickly grabbed Jamie and dragged him down the nearest passage. Granny moved swiftly across and peered through the narrow gap in the doorway.

In the study stood a man with his back to her, adjusting his collar and tie. He was facing an old marble bust. Even from a few metres away, she could see that its features were similar to those of the Hall portrait.

That was all the time she had. The sound of a cane on the flag-stones round the corner made her melt back into the crowds that were squeezing out the main doors. She found Jamie outside a short time later.

'Very dramatic,' she said. 'Superb acting.'

'Dead easy,' answered Jamie. 'I just thought of last year's mince pie.'

Biddle's speech from the front steps of Chackmore Manor was as generous as his hospitality. With one arm ostentatiously and permanently curved around the shoulder of his son, he spoke warmly and with apparently genuine feeling about the village and its inhabitants. He apologised profusely and convincingly for his initial absence from Chackmore, and also for some of the building changes at the Manor that his work forced upon him.

'Nevertheless, we will all reap the benefits of my research; this will not just be the Best-Kept Village in Buckinghamshire, but also the Best-*Funded*!' This provoked an enthusiastic burst of applause, inevitably fuelled by the copious quantities of good food and mulled wine. 'In fact, over this coming year, I will be providing a new Astroturf for the Primary school, and also bringing in a team of top interior designers to do a makeover on the village hall.' More applause, even a whistle or two. 'And now, may my son and I wish you all a wonderful Christmas and an even happier New Year!' To their reciprocated good wishes, he began to move away, before suddenly turning on his heels and raising his hands for their attention.

'I almost forgot,' he announced. 'In appreciation for your patience, support and friendship thus far, there is a small gift for each and every one of you on the way out. Sleep well, my friends!' Even more applause and clapping. A chubby man waving two large bottles started a chorus of 'For he's a jolly good fellow,' which was quickly and boozily taken up by others.

Biddle had won them over. And he knew it.

The Thompson family, like everyone else, couldn't believe the quality and personal relevance of their gifts they received at the gates. Mr Thompson was given vouchers for a course of flying lessons, his wife had been booked into a celebrity-packed 'Wreck those Wrinkles' weekend at a fabulous health spa, and Charlie was wide-eyed with astonishment at the bike – a Revelation no less.

Jamie unwrapped his present with considerable resentment but also curiosity. It turned out to be a book.

'Tough luck,' crowed Charlie.

'Hardly,' said Mr Thompson. 'That's got to be extremely valuable.'

Jamie said nothing. It was a 1726 First Edition of *Gulliver's Travels*, bound in its original polished leather and in superb condition.

He flicked through the first few pages, and noticed that most of the map had been torn out. A hand-written note lay next to it. His heart missed a beat as he quickly read the words; *'The island's gone but the people haven't. Not yet.'* He angrily screwed it up, and looked over to Granny.

She was standing under a street-light, fiddling with the tape on her present, the others standing around her.

As the paper came away, it revealed a shoebox. She gingerly lifted the lid, and then almost dropped the whole container. 'Oh my,' she exclaimed softly, and leant for support against the lamp-post

Mrs Thompson lifted it out of her trembling hands, and peered inside.

Laid out full-length was a small body.

It was male, with shoulder-length brown hair that was greying at the edges. Its clothes were a white open-necked shirt, a dark jacket, and trousers that were tucked into yellow socks.

'Perfect!' said Mrs Thompson. 'Another doll for your collection. Just what you always wanted. It's lovely.'

'She's already got one like that, Mum,' said Jamie. It was indeed a remarkable copy of Nigriff. He picked up the note at its feet. The same handwriting. *'Keep this one. The other will be mine.'*

'Well, I think he's a *very* nice man,' said Mr Thompson cheerily. 'How could he know that you had a swap? By the way, did you hear the rumour that he's the new Property Manager at Malplaquet? Could be just what the place needs.'

'Oh dear,' said Granny quietly to Jamie. She was feeling very tired, and unsteady on her feet. 'This is getting worse and worse.'

'I'm feeling sick,' said Jamie.

He was realising that he had seriously underestimated Biddle. All the previous victories of Granny and her friends now seemed to count for nothing. Those who were so intent on destroying the Lilliputians and their Empire were only just gathering their strength.

Jamie began to turn over in his mind all sorts of worrying ideas and possibilities, but of one thing he was certain.

The real campaign for Malplaquet and its people would soon begin; and he was going to have to fight much harder than ever before.

13 : The Art of Survival

'So who are you talking to this time?' asked Mrs Thompson, watching her husband sifting through mounds of photographic slides on the dining-room table. 'The Buckingham Over-60s Club? Or another WI meeting?'

'Neither,' came the reply. 'This is the big one. The North Bucks Flab-Busters.'

'Considering what happened to your waistline over Christmas,' said his wife, 'you should be *joining* them, not speaking to them.'

Mr Thompson breathed in – hard. 'That was a bit below the belt.'

'There's a lot more than a bit *above* it,' she swiftly replied. 'Presumably this talk is about Malplaquet.'

'Of course. They're organising a 'Flab-Busting Sponsored Walk' around the grounds, and they want some local background information. Ah, Jamie, perfect timing, come and have a look at this. You'll find it *very* interesting.'

Mrs Thompson disappeared, and Jamie sidled over, knowing that the last comment could also be translated as, 'Something I find interesting and you ought to as well.' His father handed him the slide viewer with an image illuminated inside. 'Remember these? We chatted about them a while ago.'

Jamie obediently peered into the box, and saw a slide of two old maps of the gardens, one above the other. The top one was very geometric – full of straight lines and sharp angles, with double rows of trees planted on the boundaries, like soldiers in battle formation. The lower map was more fluid, with wide-open spaces, gentle patches of woodland, and paths winding past softened lakes. 'Can you see the Octagon Lake at the top?'

'Yeh,' grunted Jamie. 'It's shaped like an octagon.'

'Exactly,' enthused Dad. 'And the later one, like you once said, is all wobbly.'

Jamie nodded, recalling the conversation about what he'd learnt about Malplaquet, when he had unwisely mentioned Pope's poetry. He wouldn't make that mistake again. A simple question should be harmless.

'So why did they change it?'

'Now that's a *really* interesting question. To put it another way, you want to know why early *formal* gardens became more natural, don't you?'

Jamie couldn't believe it; he'd done it again. Sensing the gathering clouds of a lecture, he mentally checked whether anything vital on TV could excuse him. Finding nothing, he had to feign interest. 'Er . . . I suppose so.'

Mr Thompson smiled, and took another deep breath (not to de-crease his waist size but to increase his brain capacity). He gestured at the slide viewer. 'This, Jamie, is the supreme example of England's greatest contribution to world art.' His son was astonished; it seemed just an ordinary plastic box, but then he realised his father meant the map images inside. 'The English Landscape Garden, the finest example of Nature and Art in harmony, has been admired and copied throughout the world – and it all began here at Malplaquet in the eighteenth century.'

'Do you mean that *top* map?' interrupted Jamie, hoping to hold back a tide of information.

'No,' said the lecturer. 'That one is an example of the earlier *formal* style. The one below, the *natural* one, is the type that was copied everywhere.'

'So why did it change?'

'For lots of reasons,' explained Mr. Thompson, 'but mainly it was the young English nobles doing the Grand Tour around Europe. It was like their Gap Year, travelling and gaining experience before settling down to a steady job back home. Italy was their most popular destination, being full of magnificent attractions.'

Jamie knew exactly what he meant. 'Like beaches, pizzas, gorgeous gir . . .'

'Hardly,' interrupted his father dismissively. 'They were cultured *gentlemen*, only interested in the *higher* pleasures – history, architecture . . . and, most importantly, *paintings*.'

'Right,' said Jamie. 'Paintings. Of course.'

'These wealthy and ambitious young men bought foreign Art by the lorry-load, especially the pictures by Poussin and Lorrain. Those two painted mythical stories of the Romans and Greeks – in the same sort of landscapes that the nobles saw in Italy. Misty hills and sparkling lakes, soft shadowy trees, and people wandering amongst classical ruins and monuments. This Art was the height of good taste – so when the travellers returned home, they hung up these souvenirs, and when they finally inherited their estates, they made their gardens look like their paintings.'

Much to his surprise, Jamie found himself understanding what his father was saying and even becoming interested. 'So when they altered Malplaquet, they weren't gardening, but doing something artistic – like building a painting?'

'Exactly!' exclaimed his father. 'Malplaquet might *seem* to be just a garden ('not recently,' thought Jamie), but it's far more than that. It's an enormous, living, breathing work of Art. But in *3D* – not 2D. Like you told me last summer, Jamie, Malplaquet is "Britain's Greatest Work of Art of the Georgian Period".'

Jamie looked stunned – which pleased Mr Thompson, who assumed his son had learnt something important.

He was right. Something incredibly important had just clicked with Jamie. He had been realising over the past months that Malplaquet was *definitely* linked with Lilliput – partly in its shape, and somehow through its temples. And now his father was saying the garden wasn't just grass, water, trees and buildings.

It was an act of artistic imagination, of creative energy.

The Lilliputians were living inside a landscape *deliberately designed to be a reminder of another country*, even another world.

A *mythical* world.

Jamie thought it wasn't surprising that Malplaquet was so mysterious. Things were now starting to make sense – or at least he knew why they *weren't* making sense. He mumbled thanks to his delighted father, and hurried upstairs to make more notes on his laptop – and to do some more thinking.

There are two types of winter in England. There are the sharp winters, with days waking to a crisp metallic light, a low sun hurting eyes and glistening on frosted roads. Hard sounds and crunching walks, and piercing night skies. It can be a precise season, with powdered snow, biting cold, the old days finishing, and promises of fresh beginnings. As surely as the leaves have perished, the new growth appears.

Then there are the muddy and murky winters, the dim days struggling to stir from the gloom, clouds sagging over the heavy land, trees slow to drop their cover, grass sinking into clogging mud, everything muted, leaden and damp. The rain clings, and the stars are in hiding. Weak snow is slush, churning to brown, and there is only a ponderous and gradual turning of the seasons. These are the dull winters that bore and drear.

And that second type was the winter that Malplaquet endured that year. Jamie and his friends wanted to take stock, to re-think their tactics against Biddle. But the grey and dull months plodded on, and their spirits suffered. Biddle's Christmas present had also made Granny very apprehensive; she spent hours worrying about Nigriff, feeling nervous whenever the little man was away for too long or was late in returning. They were all living in a time of waiting, as if everything had gone to ground.

Which in a way it had. Technically, Lilliputians don't hibernate, but they do a very good impression of doing so. If you had peered down some burrows or earthen hideaways, you might have spotted not just a family of dormice curled up for the winter, but also a collection of coloured fur coats. Tiny human faces, eyes shut and breathing gently, would be nestling amongst their folds. Of course they wouldn't stay asleep all the time, as there were jobs to be done, but those who needed their rest – like the very young and the elderly – were allowed to take it easy and dream to their hearts content. Teenagers often tried to join in the slumbering as well, but they usually received less sympathy from their parents.

Keeping warm was a constant worry for such tiny people. Some body-heat does emanate from a huddle of dormice, despite their reduced metabolic levels, but there weren't enough to go round at Malplaquet. The Provincial Assembly promised that they would re-allocate an extra dormouse to needy cases if the weather turned particularly icy, but in truth nobody really wanted to transfer a hibernating mammal from its chosen and cosy place of rest.

The only alternatives were hedgehogs, for research had shown that a single hedgehog raised air temperature in a confined space by an average of 2.3 degrees centigrade, which was better than nothing. Although it was obviously downright dangerous to cuddle up to such a prickly body, a few hardy (and thick-skinned) souls had welcomed one into their dwelling for the winter – and they did provide places for the Lilliputians to hang their clothes on to air properly.

Some families chose to spend the winter in warmer climes, and at the first severe dip in temperature they retired to either the school buildings or the garden temples that had their own heating systems. The main mansion in theory was ideal, but there were school children everywhere. Thus, as good examples of the second type of accommodation, the Queen's Temple and St Mary's Church were more suitable destinations. They were much less crowded, well-decorated and warm, and had the right mix of a traditional setting with all modern conveniences. The only real drawback was the live music.

Some of the acts were fine. In the Queen's Temple, the clarinets were mostly played to a good standard, especially by the Senior Quartet, but the trombones and trumpets (particularly when strangled by beginners) were deafening and distressing. The drum-kit (positioned in a room directly above) could literally, when being beaten into submission, make a Lilliputian bounce. The church, therefore, was better – although Wednesday, with its bell-ringing practice, was the night to be out, and the ancient organ had a most alarming sequence of cranks and wheezes. Its pump also created dust storms on the lower levels.

Thus, over the years, Granny had developed ways of keeping the tiny people warm during the winter. Apart from making and distributing armfuls of furry garments, and highly prized duvets stuffed with Malplaquet wool, she bought vast quantities of unsold charcoal from local shops at the end of every barbecue season. Then, during the bitter months of January and February (and even in a sudden cold snap in March), she would set out at dusk towards four temples, always in the same order: Friendship, the Grecian Temple, then Ancient Virtue, and finally Venus. In a darkened corner of each building, the old lady would set down a portable barbecue – a tinfoil tray full of charcoal. Occasionally she had been spotted by a random walker and given a pitiful look, but she didn't mind; she was looking after her friends. The coals lit, she moved on, knowing that once the early smoky phase had passed, and the nuggets were glowing reddish-grey, teams of Lilliputians would emerge from their homes. Carefully prising out the valuable lumps with hard wooden spears (kebab skewers), they would tip them into smaller foil sledges (from cakes and meat-pies) and drag them off to their dwellings. A good haul could keep a family warm for a few days.

Jamie enjoyed helping Granny with these tasks, although he once mystified his parents by insisting on buying a dusty bag of charcoal from Wards the Hardware Shop in town. 'It's for Granny,' he said. 'Well, for her friends. They use it in the winter.'

'Really?' said Dad. 'What for – barbecues?'

'Something like that,' said Jamie.

Apart from keeping their central heating topped up, Granny would also drop off the occasional food parcel. The Lilliputians had become extremely resourceful during their time in Malplaquet, and so each winter were used to living off nuts, berries, their supplies of grain and salted fish. Nonetheless, they found it hard to decline a nice piece of fruit cake – or cheese. These extra gifts also meant fewer raids on the larder of the National Trust café, or the school food stores, expeditions that always carried some risk. Sometimes the Lilliputians just had to queue patiently behind other scavengers – squirrels and rats – but of course there were bigger dangers. And it wasn't just the humans. Nobody ever forgot the story of Crathek, determined to bring back a Choc Ice, who had become detached from his team in the walk-in Deep Freeze. His slip down a crevasse of frost and ice in a far corner of the room had gone unnoticed, and it was years later that his stiff body, perfectly preserved and still clutching its ice axe, was found by the intrepid explorer, the great Kryasp himself.

Vicky also played her part in helping the Lilliputians this winter, admirably helped by Ralph, who was now a trusted friend. Inevitably their Trust work involved plenty of cutting back, tying up, clearing and chopping, but the ha-ha still demanded their attention. Head Office were hoping that the wall might be finished by the summer, and she and Ralph were spending days and days on it. The Head Gardener, however, didn't understand some of their techniques and designs.

'Shouldn't it be completely *solid*?' he asked one day, watching them position yet another length of piping through the wall.

'Drainage,' muttered Ralph, giving it a final shove, and looking down its length to the dark recesses behind. 'You don't want a build-up of water behind, could bring the wall down. It's what all the best ha-ha masons do nowadays.'

'But what about these cracks? Do you really need as many?'

'Ventilation' replied Vicky. 'Lets the authentic cement dry out more quickly.'

'And all that loft insulation you've stuffed behind it?'

'Comfort,' replied Ralph. 'Makes the front wall fit comfortably against the rear blocks. Trust me,' he added, 'someone could live in here by the time we've finished.'

The Head Gardener scratched his head and walked away, which meant he missed seeing the little body that popped its shoulders out of the pipe and gave a smiling thumbs-up to Ralph.

Nor did he see the wink that Ralph gave back.

And so the winter passed without major incident, with the Lilliputians remaining well hidden. A fall of snow that lasted three days could have revealed their footprints, but the people who went outside wore their special boots with soles matching the prints of birds. No human visitors suspected a thing.

One very important development, however, was that some of Nigriff's ideas about their background were being respected by a growing number of Lilliputians. During the long days sitting around lumps of charcoal, or crushing nuts and skinning berries, conversation often turned to events of the previous months, and people were becoming more open-minded about his theories.

'You can see he's absolutely convinced, totally believes it.'

'And he's got access to the documents. He ought to know his stuff.'

'Librarians aren't usually known for being crazy . . .'

'And the Guide has helped us. Like that old poem said he would.'

'Ouch! That spine's really sharp! Dad, can we have a dormouse, not a hedgehog, next year?'

'Lots of us are mixing more as well. That Yenech is spending days round at the parents of one of his team.'

'And a man called Biddle *is* the new Property Manager.'

That last fact was the most persuasive. Although they couldn't see how he might be a danger, for many it was too much of a coincidence. Clearly something was going on, and they ought at least to listen to Nigriff.

Which they duly did. In a series of well-advertised seminars over the cold and damp months, Nigriff patiently outlined his arguments and received some genuine support. '*Man and Sub-man*' was a philosophical tour-de-force, '*Island of Dreams*' was a big hit with the adventurous teenage crowd, '*Little is Beautiful*' was enjoyed at several 'Women Who Munch' gatherings, and '*The Empire Hits Back*' was a rousing portrayal of Lilliputian struggles against dark forces such as Blefuscu. As spring slowly but surely approached, Nigriff began to wonder if he might dare to be vaguely optimistic about the immediate future. Was there a chance that they could oppose and even defeat Biddle?

Was it possible after all?

Not if Snallard was typical. A young Palladian adult, he had attended several of Nigriff's talks, and had come away totally unconvinced by the evidence and arguments. He had found the Senior Imperial Archivist alarmingly narrow and limited in his views.

'The man's a *historian* by training, for goodness' sake,' he found himself thinking one day. 'He should know there are two sides to every argument. Nigriff's made Biddle out to be a complete monster. Surely the man can't be that bad.' These thoughts lead on to other conclusions. 'And I'm not sure about that Jamie either,' he mused. 'Perhaps he's only *pretending* to be our friend. His younger brother certainly looks like real trouble – almost killed Yenech and Melanak in that plane.'

Snallard therefore decided he would have to meet this Biddle himself.

On several mornings he had noticed a chauffeur-driven black car gliding up the main approach avenue, and turning left down the hill to the Trust's offices in the old Home Farm buildings. Snallard was sure it was the new Property Manager himself, doubtless coming to discuss important matters about the estate with his staff. The farm would be a good place to meet this character without any other Lilliputians knowing, for they were bound to jump to the wrong conclusions.

Snallard was understandably nervous at the thought of visiting the farm. It would mean straying beyond the garden boundaries; such wandering had never been *specifically* forbidden, but they had been fiercely discouraged by older Lilliputians, issuing all sorts of dire warnings against the idea. Nevertheless, Snallard reasoned that his mission was for the good of his people and in the interests of truth, and such high and noble motives necessarily required breaking one or two outmoded traditions. Frankly, as well, if he was really honest, he wanted to meet Biddle for himself, partly to find out for himself if the man was a villain, but also to check on Jamie's trustworthiness. If Biddle could actually *see* Snallard, all this alarming and dramatic talk about the people being visible near the temples would be a profound lie – and that would mean that Jamie, *not* Biddle, was up to no good.

With such arguments, Snallard justified his intentions.

Pleased with his plan, he waited until one bright morning he spotted the car pass by. He slipped unnoticed on a long thread down the wall of the ha-ha, trotted quickly across the road, and jogged across the field and down the hill towards the square cluster of old brick buildings.

It took him far longer than he had anticipated. The field was horribly uneven after a late ploughing, and he had to make several long detours round waterlogged ruts and ditches. It was therefore past midday when a muddy, tired and thirsty Lilliputian eventually found himself at the entrance to Home Farm's courtyard. Seeing the car parked inside to the left, he gingerly tiptoed over. Even from ground level he could see that the driver was fast asleep, head tipped back and mouth wide open. Snallard placed a weary hand on a pierced hubcap and began the climb.

Jedekiah Biddle had spent enough time with his staff for one day. It had been fairly productive, with details checked for the spectacular 'Spring Opening' event, and more plans finalised for the rest of the summer. Things were shaping up very nicely; he was almost feeling pleased. He paused at the top of the steps leading out of his office, loosened his tie, and glanced across at his car. His affable mood was spoilt by the sight of his slumbering driver. It was the second time it had happened; the man was clearly useless, and would have to go.

This rising anger, however, was rapidly replaced by a mixture of shock, bewilderment and delight.

There was no mistaking it. Sat on the front of the car's bonnet was a tiny figure. It was taking off its shoes and banging them together.

Jedekiah knew immediately that it was a Lilliputian; it had to be. But how could he see it so clearly? For years he'd never been able to see anything more than their vague outlines and misty shapes – thus needing to depend so much on that fool Newbold. But *this* one was as real and as solid as . . . well, as himself.

Biddle could barely contain his surprise and excitement, but with deliberate and quiet steps he strode over towards his car. He was now hoping that the driver *wouldn't* wake up.

As soon as Biddle had appeared by the door, Snallard had sensed the man's authority and power, and when he then began to walk over, he tried not to feel nervous. As a youngster he too had been told the stories of the 'Biddleman,' and this human might yet be linked with it in some way. But he looked so smart and efficient, so competent – how could he be that evil?

Snallard was already close to deciding that both Nigriff and Jamie were deceiving them all, and when a large open hand was stretched out in a friendly greeting, with one finger extended, the first words absolutely settled the matter.

'Good day, allow me to introduce myself. My name is Jedekiah Biddle, the Lord of the Manor of Chackmore, and also the new Property Manager of Malplaquet. I can only say that I'm *enormously* delighted to see you.'

Snallard immediately grasped the finger, shook it firmly, and knew deep down that he would be doing business with this impressive man. That oh-so-clever Nigriff would sooner or later be revealed as both a fool and a liar.

14 : Visions of the Past and Future

At the end of the second term, Jamie brought home his report.

'Oh good,' exclaimed Mrs Thompson, eagerly tearing open the envelope. 'I've been waiting for this. All those ticked boxes last Christmas didn't tell me anything. Rather like my eldest son. . . .'

'I think you'll be pleased with it,' said Jamie. 'Start with Science.'

His parents were seated together on the sofa. 'I see what you mean,' said his father after a while. 'Physics; *lots of energy and is a force for good.* Biology; *the whole class continues to evolve well.* And the Chemistry teacher says elements of your work have been excellent. That sounds fine.'

'Maths is good,' said Mum. '*All adds up to a pleasing start.*'

'Games is a bit funny,' said his father. '*Undoubtedly talented and is controlling earlier bouts of aggression.* What's all that about?'

'Hockey last term,' confessed Jamie. 'This kid kept annoying me.'

'Which one?' asked Dad.

'John Biddle.'

'But John's a *lovely* lad,' said Mum. 'He's been a good friend to Charlie, and his father has been so kind to people in the village. That Christmas party . . .'

'Can we go back to my report?' said Jamie, becoming exasperated.

His parents exchanged glances and then his father read on. 'Visual Education; *outstanding. The second-best student in the year.* So who's the best?'

'It doesn't matter,' grumbled Jamie.

'Right, I see,' said Dad.

'*Loves drawing local maps and enjoyed our recent project on islands,*' said Mum. 'The Geography teacher seems happy.'

'So does Art and Design,' agreed Dad. '*Growing interest in the works of Poussin and Lorrain.* Well, that's nice to know. *Model-making skills superb.*'

'They should be,' said Mum, 'after all those hours with bits of cardboard. Now, what about RS? *Fascinated by ancient myths; has a sensitive appreciation of the mysteries of Nature.*' She paused. 'Presumably this means the gardens?'

'Probably,' replied Jamie.

'History isn't that great,' said Dad. '*Has learnt much about life in the eighteenth century. Unfortunately we have been studying the rise of Hitler.*'

'I did that as well . . .'

'English say you're a *wide and imaginative reader* – which is good,' said Mum, 'and you *enjoy Alexander Pope* – no surprise there – *Jonathan Swift, and the novels of T H White.* That's a bit of an odd mix, isn't it? Why them?'

'Why not?' said Jamie. 'They're all great writers.'

His parents had no answer for that, and overall were pleased that their son was having a promising first year. He was obviously learning a great deal.

On the first Friday in April, the *Buckingham and Winslow Advertiser* published a Special Supplement on 'What To Do and Where To Go this Easter.' It included an article with the headline, 'Local Gardens Spring Into Life?' It read as follows.

Malplaquet, the local world-famous garden owned by the National Trust, has always excited its visitors. But a new craze has really caught their imagination – called 'Spot the Moving Statues.'

The game began last autumn, when an old lady wrote to the

Trust to complain about the Temple of British Worthies and its 'moving eyes.' She described 'this attempt to amuse tourists' as 'misguided and creepy.' Her concern was properly investigated, and the letter put to one side as a harmless prank. The fun really began when two walkers in February asked a Volunteer how the Trust managed to get George I's horse to snort so realistically. The very next day a teenage girl was heard describing the moving turtle in the Grecian Temple's pediment.

The stories have multiplied like wildfire in recent weeks, and the Trust suspect that it's all been hyped up by mobile phones and text messaging. Certainly there are many people visiting Malplaquet with either a wonderful sense of fun, appalling eyesight, or over-active imaginations. Only today, one gentleman claimed that he had nearly been abducted by the beautiful Venus de Medici in the Rotonda; his wife responded, 'In your dreams,' and hurried him off home. The latest reported sighting is the female figure on top of the Grenville Column happily singing an operatic aria.

The Advertiser asked Mr. Jedekiah Biddle, the Property Manager at Malplaquet, for his thoughts on the issue.

'People have always been inspired here,' he said, 'such as the great names of the eighteenth century – Pope, Walpole, Capability Brown, even Catherine the Great of Russia – or more recently T H White with his Mistress Masham's Repose. *One's creative instincts are fired by these magical gardens; it's the way the temples interact with the landscape, or the special light, or even the shadows. It's undoubtedly a tribute to the original designers, but also to our excellent team of restorers, who are doing fabulous work. They have made the place come alive for our thousands of visitors. I'm glad people find Malplaquet so enjoyable and entertaining – but I'm afraid I'm late for a chat with Homer in Ancient Virtue. If your readers want a really good story . . .'*

Clearly there's much happening at Malplaquet, and Mr. Biddle's light-hearted and welcoming approach seems to be paying off. The full details of the Easter Opening Times and Events – culminating in the Napoleonic Association weekend – are printed below.'

Seated in his study at Chackmore, the Lord of the Manor was pleased with the article. The personal compliment at the end was most satisfying and helpful, but it was all valuable publicity for his estate. He was determined to massively increase the number of visitors, especially if they would prowl round all sorts of hidden corners and use their eyes carefully. Flush the Lilliputians out, that was his plan: make their life in the gardens miserable. Help them to realise that J Thompson had upset their life last summer, and that a local benefactor was offering them somewhere to live that was more secure and more clinical. A place where they could be really useful.

Jedekiah Biddle had no idea, of course, which crackpot had started these tales of living sculptures, but he had rapidly seen their marketing value. He particularly enjoyed the 'operatic statue' story he himself had contributed. And next week a man with a walking-stick would hobble to the pay-desk to give a wild-eyed account (with a Scots accent) of the monkey atop the Congreve Monument, which was combing its hair and staring at its mirror. Highly amusing, and a useful addition to the campaign. He knew he could trust the gullible public to make up a few more themselves.

He sat back in his leather armchair, reflecting on his recent meeting with Snallard. If all Lilliputians were that stupid, it was going to be ridiculously easy. He suspected from events so far that they weren't, but this first one was an absolute pushover. Biddle had found no difficulty in gaining the complete trust of the little man, nor in finding out his passion for marzipan.

The difference in brain-power was embarrassing. Biddle smirked, recalling how rapidly Snallard had believed that Nigriff (whom Newbold had marked as the key Lilliputian, hence the Christmas doll) wanted to become a *Permanent Listener*, in effect a new Emperor with limitless powers. 'Only courageous and independent people, Snallard, can prevent these selfish ambitions from damaging your countrymen.' Those had been his closing words, with a warning to tell no-one of their meeting, 'in case Nigriff finds out and tries to harm the country's saviour.'

In the quiet of his study, Jedekiah Biddle laughed out loud. 'What fools these pathetic creatures are!' he thought. 'Now, what can I tell him next time we meet?'

'I'm not at all sure about this,' said Granny, standing nervously in front of the Pebble Alcove. She looked accusingly in turn at Jamie and Vicky on either side – and also at Nigriff, who was peering out of Vicky's shoulder-bag. It was early evening, and the cooling air was encouraging slow ribbons of mist to gather on the lake behind them.

'There's nothing to be afraid of, Granny,' said Jamie, trying to reassure her. 'We've all been in here before, including you. Remember the Mermaid?'

'Yes, but I just thought you were imagining things then,' she replied. 'Once I knew it really *did* show you pictures, I've not been in since. I'm not sure it's safe.'

'We might not see anything anyway,' said Jamie. 'That happened to me once. It might not work properly again.'

'All the more reason for *not* going in,' she remarked tersely. 'And anyway, if it does work, all you three say it's bits from the Gulliver story. I could read the book again instead . . . I'll 'see' better pictures in that, than watching something on a screen in here. People nowadays, new technology turns up, and before you know it . . .'

'Madam, this is not new, but *old* technology,' sniffed Nigriff, hurt at the slight to this remarkable visual archive. 'Tried and tested.'

'And trusted,' added Jamie. 'Look, the point is that it's been showing us what we *need* to know, not just anything we dream up. Come on, Granny, it'll be fun, I'll look after you.' He took hold of her hand and coaxed her forward. Granny turned to Vicky, and found some sympathy in her eyes. The teenager knew how hard it was for the elderly to adjust to the modern – or, in this case, the ancient – world. She took Granny's other hand, and in a line they entered the Alcove, turned as one, and hand-in-hand sat down on the inner bench.

A slight breeze suddenly lifted across the waters, swirling the hovering mist and curling it into denser folds. The air cooled slightly. Jamie and Vicky turned to inspect the curved walls and the inlaid designs, and Nigriff tried to clamber out of the bag. Granny, her shoulders hunched and her eyes half-shut, squinted nervously at the nearest pattern. She had decided that the cow was probably the safest bet.

'Do you know,' said Vicky slowly, breaking the silence, 'I never noticed that there were so many things from nature here. A dragon-fly . . . rabbit . . . a flower. . . .'

'You're right,' agreed Jamie. 'The sun . . . a star . . . a crescent moon . . .'

Only when they talked about it afterwards did they realise that just at that precise moment, when Jamie was describing those patterns from Outer Space, Vicky was lifting Nigriff out of her bag. All four of them therefore were holding hands, all linked together. That was exactly when they noticed the light suddenly fading, and the mist not just blocking their view but effectively sealing them in the Alcove.

Jamie and Vicky felt Granny's hands tighten, as the light inside turned to a soft grey, with cool wafts of air still blowing across their faces but not at all disturbing the damp fog. Jamie glanced at the others; Nigriff was standing on Vicky's open hand, his eyes wide-open in anticipation. She was calm, slightly smiling. Granny had both her eyes shut and was breathing slowly and deliberately.

'Don't worry,' Jamie whispered. 'This is what it usually does.'

And then it did what it had never done before. As Jamie looked at the patterns, he saw that they were glowing slightly, providing small pools of light in the temple. Light of various colours, matching the pebbles – chocolate browns, creamy whites, sea-greens. Not only that, but the walls had faded away, leaving the luminous stones floating amongst a deep blackness – and from all around began the swelling of a gentle murmur, a quiet lilting dream of a sound. Not a human voice, nor an instrument, but something that felt older, from the depths of creation itself. 'Like waves of golden wheat flowing across a windswept hill,' was Granny's description later. 'It was beautiful; I wanted to cry and be happy at the same time.'

The sweet and haunting melody gradually grew stronger and louder, and as it did so the mist before them parted. Far below – for they now seemed hundreds of feet in the air – was the unmistakeable shape of Malplaquet, with its lakes, woods, and temples, as clear as in full daylight. It was encircled by a low and continuous bank of cloud, exactly like an island emerging from a sea-mist. Its colours were vibrant, almost fluorescent (especially the green of the grass), and the whole landscape was glowing from within, pulsating with life and energy.

'My word!' uttered Granny, still hanging on to Vicky and Jamie, especially as she assumed that they were somehow airborne. 'That's worth coming to see.'

'Have you noticed the pebbles?' asked Vicky, to no-one in particular. 'They're going backwards.'

Expanding, but retaining their particular shapes, and shining ever more brightly the further they travelled, they were receding into the darkness – and never simply in a direct line, but reacting and adjusting to each other, as if in a stately dance. In less than half a minute, the four travellers found themselves weightlessly suspended in the midst of a night sky, illuminated by glittering galaxies and a crescent moon, and charmed by the music of this new universe. They were entranced and spellbound. No-one, not even Granny, felt afraid, and no-one wanted it to end.

Nigriff was the first to voice his thoughts. 'My friends,' he said, looking around him, 'I should have realised years ago.' He began pointing out some of the magnificent constellations glistening around them. 'Vacca – the cow. Papilio – the butterfly. Flos – the flower. Pisces – the fish.' He swallowed hard, struggling to find the words. When he did there was a hushed tone to his voice.

'This glorious panoply is like the very vault of heaven; it is none other than the night sky of Lilliput itself.'

He bowed his head as the sanctity of the place sank in, and as he did so the coloured stars shone even more brilliantly, browns turning to copper-golds, blues to silver and pearl, the vast canopy shot through with a dazzling display of emeralds and rubies and sapphires. The music of the stars was still playing, encouraging a deeper colour and richness to each changing light. The travellers gazed open-mouthed at the unfolding spectacle, conscious of its awesome beauty and immensity.

It was the sudden gasp from Nigriff that startled the others.

He was staring straight ahead, one hand over his mouth, and his whole body trembling. While they had been fascinated by the celestial glories above and around them, the 'island' of Malplaquet had been undergoing a transformation.

Its shape had hardly altered, but it now had become a true island, surrounded by a glassy sea, presided over by a noble walled city. Its rolling landscape was full of well-kept fields and green pastures, quiet waters, majestic woods, and neat dwellings for its people.

There was no mistaking its identity. No-one wished to speak, but the three humans were all aware of Nigriff, who was lost in quiet contemplation of the scene. Jamie noticed tears forming in Granny's eyes, and gently squeezed her hand.

A vision such as this cannot remain forever, and the image soon began to fade, but none of those present could ever say whether it had lasted for seconds or minutes, or even hours. But the memory of it stayed with them for the rest of their days.

As it withdrew from their sight, the pebbles shrank inwards to set into their cement walls. The music drifted away, the air chilled, and all things became hushed. Trails of mist parted in front of the alcove, unveiling a lake-side and a darkening April evening. A duck came gliding in across the water, splashing and sliding to an ungainly halt.

Even after they had let go of each other's hands and stood up to stretch themselves, nobody uttered a word. It was a very thoughtful, even mournful, group that made its way back along the wooded path to the cottage. The experience had been both humbling and uplifting; yet their sense of distance from that priceless country was now profound.

Especially for one of them. Nigriff now knew that Lilliput was real, but was utterly, impossibly, out of reach. He had been given a glimpse of an unattainable happiness. Joy and sadness merged in the little man's heart.

Furthermore, little did they suspect at that moment, but as they subsequently discovered whenever they tried to repeat this experience, never again would the Pebble Alcove open up its mysteries to them. It had done its job, completed its task; it had prepared their hearts and minds.

From now on they would have to trust in other powers and rely upon other strengths.

And they would certainly need them.

As the sun was setting, Snallard rode on squirrel-back for his first ever visit to the Bourbon Tower. A single robust castle tower, the ruin stood alone in a windswept field just to the east of Malplaquet. It looked forbidding and intimidating, and Snallard sensed his own nervousness and that of the squirrel beneath him as they approached. They both were very wary of this territory beyond the garden.

Pulling to a halt outside the gaping door frame, Snallard gave instructions to his mount to wait, and gingerly stepped into the darkened interior. Immediately he heard the animal outside scurry away. Snallard cursed under his breath, and picked his way through the rubble and rusty cans towards the wooden staircase that circled the room, his heart thudding firmly. Reaching the bottom step, he hauled himself up. Although not far apart, the treads were open, giving a grim view as he ascended.

He felt he would have stopped if it hadn't been for the justice of his cause.

Finally emerging on the flat roof, he was relieved to see a figure standing silhouetted against the parapet, looking out over the landscape. Without turning round it announced, 'Well done, my friend, you have yet again proved your worth and courage. A pity your dumb animals lack such qualities.' Biddle turned on his heels, beckoned Snallard over, and sat down on the low wall.

'We can talk safely here. Now for your reward.' He reached inside his coat and pulled out a small and bulging paper bag. 'Made by Wiltshire's,' he stated. 'The best. From the West Country.' Snallard opened the bag eagerly, and gasped at the small marzipan fruits inside – cherries, bananas, limes, strawberries, all beautifully crafted and each one a meal in itself. Biddle watched his ally begin to tear one apart and stuff the confection in his mouth. 'When you've finished one, tell me what you think I should know.'

Biddle couldn't believe his luck that this Lilliputian was so stupid – and also so talkative, for in the next ten minutes he divulged plenty of good information. For example, Jamie Thompson had been introduced to the people last summer as the new assistant to the old lady in the Bell Gate Cottage, who needed help in looking after them. But the boy had been trouble from the start. He'd changed their big contest, upset some local golfers, and almost allowed two of Snallard's people to be captured by a disgusting human. 'Appalling,' had been Biddle's reaction. 'Very careless.' Then there was the invisibility issue.

'None of us have ever understood it,' said Snallard, eyeing up a banana, 'but few humans have ever been able to see us. Then Thompson turns up, and he and Nigriff say we can't go near the temples because they make us visible.'

'Hmm,' replied Biddle, intrigued. 'But that's where you *live*, isn't it?'

'Right!' exclaimed Snallard. 'I'm glad *someone* understands that.'

'It sounds to me,' said Biddle, thinking fast, 'as if he wants you to stay in the open. Suspicious, don't you think?' Snallard nodded repeatedly, his mouth full. 'It's a clever ploy,' said Biddle, 'but untrue, because I first saw you *nowhere near* a temple.'

'*Precisely*,' agreed Snallard. 'And there's this rubbish about Lilliput.' Biddle became even more attentive, listening hard. 'Nigriff has managed to convince a few people about his ideas, even Professor Malowit I think, but there's *no way* we came from an island across the seas. It's obviously just a story.'

'You're right,' said Biddle, trying to sound impressed. 'You've rumbled their plans. Nigriff clearly wants power for himself . . .' He paused, watching the anger on Snallard's face. 'But Thompson is your *main* enemy. It's fiendishly clever,' he muttered. 'He wants you all to dream of a distant homeland (which of course you can never reach) and so not notice the misery he's inflicting upon you. He might even delude some into thinking that the only way to get there is to obey him. I can imagine what will happen,' he added grimly. 'One by one, people will disappear from the garden, never to be seen again. You'll be told they're in Lilliput, blissfully happy.'

'Would he really do that?' interrupted Snallard, finding it hard to accept such wickedness, and not wanting to hear any more details.

'There are such people,' said Biddle. 'And from what we know of Thompson so far . . .' He shook his head sadly.

'We have to stop them,' exclaimed Snallard angrily. 'All of them, including the two females!'

'The old lady and . . ?' inquired Biddle, wanting his earlier information verified.

'Vicky; she works with the Volunteers.'

'The very one,' said Biddle. He thought for a few seconds. 'We'll meet here again, tomorrow. Same time. I can give you a lift downstairs – but no further. My car is waiting in the lane, and we cannot be seen together. It wouldn't be safe for you.'

Snallard agreed, pleased to be with a man who had the best interests of himself and his people at heart. He twisted the top of the bag, and was looking forward to a snack on the long and dark walk home, until Biddle said, 'I need to keep those. You would not be able to explain where they came from.'

'Of course,' said Snallard. He tried to ignore the sudden feeling of disappointment and loneliness. His increasing stomach-ache wasn't comfortable either; greed always was his big problem.

'Like taking candy from a baby,' said Biddle later to his henchman, both hunched over the chess set in his study. 'Or I should say, giving sweets to a midget.' The other man laughed quietly and obediently. 'Moreover,' continued Biddle, 'I may have already found the perfect recipe for success.'

'What's that, sir?' came the required response.

'Noises apparently. Fireworks, loud explosions, bangs. Gets them upset, they can't cope. Some hide, others get caught in the open, totally confused and disorientated. Remind me; what *is* our major holiday event at Malplaquet?' He already knew the answer, but wanted to relish the reply.

'It's a military re-enactment, sir, the Napoleonic Association.'

'Likely to be noisy? Cannons, rifles, musket-fire? Gunpowder perhaps?' The sarcasm in his voice was easy to detect, and his words were met with a wry grin.

'I thought as much. This little conflict will be embarrassingly one-sided. Especially when Napoleon discovers that his army has suddenly received an influx of highly-experienced recruits. Now, who shall we contact? Let me think . . .'

The chess was pushed to one side, as Biddle had lost interest. His opponent quickly and properly acknowledged his master's superior position.

Jedekiah, the Lord of the Manor of Chackmore, the Property Manager of Malplaquet, and the proud descendant of the great sea-captain, John Biddle, now had another contest that needed immediate planning.

He had every confidence of winning that one as well.

Checkmate.

15 : Hawkwell Field

At Malplaquet it had been one of those heartening April days when summer seems just around the corner – plants budding, the smell of cut grass, and relaxed visitors in shirt-sleeves ambling through the gardens. Four friends, just returned from an extraordinary trip in the Pebble Alcove, were sat in the western Lake Pavilion, enjoying the gentle warmth of the late afternoon sun. Their recent experience had affected all of them, but Nigriff was feeling it more keenly than anybody else.

'All I know,' he announced, breaking into their deliberations, 'is that henceforth I must live in a way that honours that glorious and distant country.'

'It *was* awesome,' agreed Jamie. 'Especially when the gardens changed into the island – best special effects *I've* ever seen. It also shows we're dead right about a link between Malplaquet and Lilliput.'

'Not being funny or anything,' said Vicky, sat on the end of the line, 'but we are *totally* sure that was Lilliput, are we?' Three reproving faces turned towards her. 'Okay, fair enough, of course it was. But I did wonder – just briefly – if we all imagined it, y'know, mass hysteria or something.'

'That island was, without a shadow of a doubt, the *least* imaginary thing I have ever witnessed, Miss Vicky,' responded Nigriff firmly.

'And I don't think any of us were hysterical,' said Jamie.

'I was a bit, to be honest,' confessed Vicky. 'Back home later, when I realised I'd been floating around an unknown galaxy on a tatty park bench.'

'Could be a new hobby,' suggested Jamie. 'Inter-galactic space travel. It would look great on your University application.'

'Now there's an idea,' said Granny. 'People say it's good to have something to make your application stand out. That would do nicely.'

The mood was lightening, even though they still had a few questions about their Cosmic Awayday. Nigriff brought them back down to earth.

'Should we be concerned about this weekend's military re-enactment? Is this another battle from the prophecy, planned by our enemy?'

'I shouldn't think it was Biddle's idea,' said Jamie. 'It must have been dreamt up ages ago, before he got the job. But we'll have to be careful; you never can tell with him.'

'You'll be here, won't you, Jamie?' asked Granny.

He nodded. 'Charlie has been asked to be a drummer-boy, so Mum and Dad want to see him all dressed-up. It could be hilarious.'

'Do the Lilliputians realise there'll be a lot of noise?' said Granny.

'Thorclan's on to it,' said Vicky. 'He's holding a large meeting soon. He's getting quite excited about it all. I don't know what his plans are.'

'Oh dear,' said Granny. 'Sorry, I really meant, oh good.'

In the Grecian Temple, Thorclan cast his eyes over the volunteers and troops seated before him. The response to his call to arms had been impressive, and he was honestly surprised at the number of potential soldiers in the other three provinces. Nonetheless, he detected an air or apprehension, of nervousness. He knew to expect this the night before a major battle – and Napoleonic armies did have a decent reputation.

He looked to either side along the platform, his heart swelling with pride. On his immediate right sat Gniptip, his trusted and sharp PA, shuffling papers. Next were Trimter, then Humelish, and lastly the new TQS – Wesel, Hyroc, Melanak and Yenech. The last pair were engaged in deep conversation, smiling at each other. Thorclan instinctively knew they would be discussing tactical manoeuvres. On the General's left were Cherbut, Hamnob, Yassek, and finally Sevegar and Raida, both promoted after their Cold Stream Cup exploits.

Thorclan smoothed his uniform, nudged Gniptip, and rose to his feet. His PA tapped the table loudly, and the room fell silent, all eyes on the speaker. He cleared his throat and began, choosing his sombre words carefully for maximum dramatic effect.

'Today is one day, and tomorrow will be another day. A day unlike any other day. In that day, tomorrow, you will remember this day, today, and call it . . . *yesterday*. And today I say that tomorrow will one day seem like yesterday, when in old age you relive this day, and say, "That was the day, the day I became what I am today." *Tomorrow* is that day.'

It was stirring stuff. All the Grecians knew to applaud enthusiastically, although other provincials, unused to such high rhetoric, just looked at each other.

'And now,' continued the General, 'allow me to introduce on my left my right-hand man, Cherbut, who will give you an idea of the enemy's strength.'

The young officer got to his feet, hurriedly pulling a notebook from an inside pocket. 'The usual weapons of the Napoleonic armies are as follows,' he announced, reading off the page. 'First, the Infantry. Muskets: three rounds a minute, accurate up to 70 human paces. Rifles: they fire a spinning lead ball, accurate up to 200 paces. Bayonets. Swords. Nine-foot pikes. And Pistols.' He detected an awkward shuffling in the audience, but was encouraged by Thorclan's positive words to continue. 'Good show, Cherbut, don't stop now. Let them have it.'

'Now the Cavalry,' he intoned. 'Two types. Heavy, for breaking up tight formations, and Light, for patrolling and reconnaissance. Swords, curved or straight-sided. The French have *excellent* lancers.' A noticeable unease was spreading.

'Finally, the Artillery. The cannons and howitzers fire cannonballs, three to twelve pounds in weight. Also case-shot: tin containers of small lead balls that explode apart on leaving the barrel. And sometimes they fire shells: again, canisters of lead pellets, but with a fuse timed to burst over the enemy's heads.' Numbers of people were moving towards the door, shaking their heads. The General, from his years of army leadership, had expected exactly that response. He leapt to his feet.

'Is *that* all they've got?' he bellowed. 'Is that the *best* they can do?' His words and air of confidence had the desired effect; people turned to look. He adopted a swaggering pose, like a man laughing in the face of impossible odds. He laughed quietly. 'Let me make something clear,' he began. 'Cherbut, did these armies ever use those deadly white missiles of the MiGs?'

Cherbut looked surprised. 'You mean those golf balls, General?'

Thorclan nodded. 'The very same.'

Cherbut confirmed his general's suspicions. 'No, sir. Napoleon's armies never used golf balls.'

'*There* you are!' barked Thorclan triumphantly. 'Shows how tactically *naïve* they are! And let me tell you one other thing, my good men . . .'

'. . . and women,' added Gniptip.

'. . . the fact is this lot never actually fire *anything* anyway! No cannonballs, no lead shot. There's just noise and lots of smoke.'

His troops did seem relieved. Thorclan pressed home his advantage. 'Trimter, what's our *normal* reaction to noise and smoke?'

'We run and hide, General.'

Thorclan was taken aback. Gniptip swiftly handed him a document. 'It says here,' Thorclan read, 'that we should "*make a considered, positive and immediate response.*" Isn't that correct?'

'Yes, sir. We *consider* running and hiding. Then we *positively* do it. *Immediately.*'

'Well, tomorrow we won't,' said Thorclan bluntly.

A hand shot up from the front. 'General, aren't these humans fighting *each other*, even if they are pretending? Why are *we* involved – and whose side are we on?'

'Our side,' replied the great strategist. 'The idea is to cause havoc, make both sides retreat, show them the power of the whole Provincial Army. Stop them using this place so much. Good plan, eh?'

'What about their horses?' interrupted another voice. '*They're* not pretend ones. What have we got? Squirrels?'

'You'll be glad to know that "yes" is the answer,' replied Thorclan. 'But not *just* squirrels. And here's some more good news. For the first time ever, I've ignored basic army tactics and allowed the enemy to choose the terrain. But they've made a *huge* mistake, and chosen the

Hawkwell Field. It's nowhere near any temples. If the temples *do* make us visible, they won't affect us there. And the grass is so long we'd be hidden anyway. We've also got plenty of camouflage, haven't we, Trimter?'

'Not *plenty*, General. It was recently washed and hung out to dry on some bushes - and we can't find most of it.'

Despite that minor difficulty, Thorclan's overall grasp of the situation was reassuring, and he talked long into the night about his plans. As the companies eventually left for home under a crescent moon, there was an air of optimism and excitement. Whatever Thorclan had said, it had achieved the desired effect.

Next morning at Malplaquet, Mrs Thompson had a poor start to her first Napoleonic battle. Opening the door to exit a blue Portaloo cubicle in the spectator area, she found herself staring down the wrong end of six muskets. A line of the King's German Legion, kneeling in dark green uniforms only ten metres away, were regarding the convenience as a major threat and had it in their sights. Mrs Thompson leapt back in, slammed the door, and waited for the volley of shots. Three seconds later all six men shouted 'bang!' in unison, and the cubicle's lone inhabitant breathed a sigh of relief. She slipped away while they were reloading. The Battle of Portaloo had fortunately not become another Waterloo.

Mrs Thompson wanted to take some photos of Charlie looking smart in his drummer's outfit (he and his friend John had been called up by Mr Biddle, who had kindly supplied all the necessary gear, including the hardwood drums). So with Mr Thompson by her side, they were picking their way through the rows of robust white canvas tents, set up on Friday evening to provide authentic accommodation for all the participants. Stepping around log fires with black cooking pots perched on open metal frames, they watched a group of men and women pouring dark gunpowder through funnels into paper cartridges. Elsewhere, British and French flags were jammed in the ground, soldiers in a variety of colourful woollen uniforms stood chatting, and an important-looking man, wearing the British red jacket and white crossbelts, was advising two new recruits. Clearly at their first event, they were nervous and self-conscious in their stiff and heavy outfits. 'Don't worry,' he was saying, '*relax*. If you get hot and tired in the battle, pretend you've been shot and just fall over.'

Mrs Thompson shielded her eyes and spotted two young drummers emerging from between the bouncy castle and the white caravan entitled 'Hogroast.'

'Good, there they are. I wonder how they got on last night.'

'They'll have been fine,' said her husband. 'This bunch are harmless.'

'Harmless, apart from being armed to the teeth,' said Mrs Thompson. 'Hello, chaps. You do look smart, especially with that black cap thing.'

'Shako,' said Charlie.

'I beg your pardon?'

'It's the name for the cap,' said John. 'Our jackets are called red rags.'

'They taught us some proper words last night,' said Charlie.

'Excellent,' said Dad. 'Glad you're into the spirit of it. How was the food?'

'The skilly was yucky, but the stirrabout and the pong were okay,' said John.

'Not forgetting the bumper of belch,' added Charlie.

'And the knock-me-down in the blackjack,' said John.

The two adults stared blankly at each other.

'Don't worry, Mr Thompson, we kept off the stingo and bishop,' said John.

'And the rumbo and bumbo,' said Charlie.

Mrs Thompson had heard enough. 'Right you two. Go and do your battle thing, and come back when you can talk some sense.' The parents strode off to find a couple of seats with a good view of the conflict across the stretch of water.

Charlie looked at John. 'What do you reckon about her?'

'Yeh, definitely. Baggage.'

'Just a bitch booby,' said Charlie.

'Remind me again, guv'nor, whose clobber's this?'

Biddle stifled a groan. He looked at the dozen hired men drooped around the tent, and regretted promising to pay them so much. 'That, my friend, is the splendid uniform of Napoleon's Imperial Guard.' That statement was entirely accurate. From the polished knee-high black boots and white trousers, to the dark blue great coat with its white facings and wide red cuffs, all surmounted by a bearskin sporting a red plume, the outfit was the height of military elegance. 'You are now the elite fighting force of the French Army.' That final statement was much less accurate.

'Oh, yeah, now I remember. I knew that was us.'

Another spoke up, slowly, with a thick rural accent. 'What's the plan again?'

Biddle was trying to be patient; he needed their personal loyalty, just as Napoleon had done. 'Stay by the French Artillery.' A hand went up. 'That means *cannons*,' explained Biddle. The hand went down. 'Then, on my signal, run to the nearby temples and start looking around.'

'What for?'

'Anything about six inches high.'

'Like a squirrel? They're mostly that size.'

'No,' replied Biddle sharply, getting frustrated but not wanting to say too much. 'Not a squirrel. Something unusual.'

'Mr. Biddle, 'ow about a squirrel *doin'* summat unusual? I once saw one wiv a golf ball, an' it was . . .'

'No!' shouted Biddle. '*No* squirrels! Of any kind . . . doing anything . . . ! Don't go anywhere near them!' He clenched his fists in exasperation. Why did he keep meeting stupid people? These thoughts were interrupted by a whistle and a shout from outside. 'All companies report to their officers!' The elite fighting force trooped sullenly out, grumbling amongst themselves.

'It's money wot's dun it,' said one. 'Gone to his 'ead. Thinks he's Napoleon.'

Seated on white plastic chairs or sprawled in canvas deckchairs, the crowds of spectators were tucking into their picnics and various items of Fast Food. Across the river, lazily flowing from under the Palladian Bridge to their right, a re-enactment of an early nineteenth-century battle was taking place.

Deployed in the Hawkwell Field, which sloped gently up to the Gothic Temple and its clumps of trees, were disparate groups of colourful soldiers, mostly red and white, but some in dark blue or green. Puffs of smoke wafted around, as the participants marched about or stood in lines, occasionally kneeling to let out a 'crack' from their musket.

Flags were being paraded, teams of men were pulling cannon into position, the occasional body keeled over, and a few cavalry officers were trotting about on their steeds. It was a very gentlemanly conflict. The commentary, barely audible through a small loudspeaker, tried to explain what was happening, such as 'the Light Infantry are pushing forward,' or 'they're in skirmish order,' and 'the commanders need to watch their flanks.'

'Don't we all,' murmured a large lady spectator, holding a burger.

Mr and Mrs Thompson particularly enjoyed watching two drummer boys march across the bridge with their detachment. 'That's my son,' said Mrs Thompson proudly to her neighbour. 'Only joined up yesterday.' Mr Thompson was less impressed with the performance of the King's German Rifles, who were collapsing in alarming numbers. His wife noticed them as well. 'Can't say I'm surprised,' she said. 'It took six of them to defeat a Portaloo this morning.' Her husband knew this was something not to ask about.

Close enough for foraging and yet far enough away to avoid embarrassment, sat Jamie, scanning the field with his binoculars. Granny and Vicky were in the GT next to him, enjoying the shade and the comfortable seats.

'It would have been nice for Ralph to have seen this,' said Granny, 'but he said he had lots of rubbish to burn. And don't Charlie and John look smart?'

'*Very* pretty,' agreed Jamie smugly.

'The cannon are absolutely real,' crackled the loudspeaker. 'Keep your mouths open to equalise the pressure . . . they're just about to fire . . . not real shot of course.'

'Cool,' said Jamie, swinging his binoculars round. 'That's the Imperial Guard over there. They're the best.'

'The famous Imperial Guards,' continued the announcer, 'adding a touch of class to our re-enactment, have kindly been supplied by Mr Biddle, the Property Manager of Malplaquet. On your behalf, could I thank him for his generosity?' A ripple of applause came from the spectators, and was acknowledged by a brief wave from a figure who suddenly appeared from behind the parapet of the bridge.

'So that's where he is,' said Vicky.

'He's up to something,' said Jamie. 'He's not hired those soldiers just for fun.'

'I think he's still trying to impress people,' said Granny. 'I mean, he can't harm our little friends today. The bangs are no worse than normal fireworks, and there's hardly anything happening anyway.'

Which of course is entirely the wrong thing to say.

Everything became different from that moment onwards.

The red-coated British had just formed a classic square, each side defended by kneeling soldiers, their muskets rammed into the ground, bayonets at an intimidating angle. Behind them stood a line of men rapidly firing and loading, and in the centre stood a major, three of his officers, the flags – and two well-dressed drummer boys. Some French cavalry were prancing around the square, waving their swords to look menacing.

Vicky noticed it first. 'Where's all that smoke coming from?' The trees on the left were already shrouded in dense grey billows, drifting through the foliage and swirling across the field.

'I'd suggest a man with a bonfire,' said Granny. 'Like Ralph?'

'I'd suggest a man with a plan,' said Jamie. 'A little General. Like Napoleon.'

The forming of that British square had been the signal. A group of Lilliputian fencers had scurried across the field and, completely unseen, had taken up their pre-arranged positions just behind the towering figures of the kneeling front-line troops. Tense, but highly-trained, they were now listening for the command from the British officer.

They didn't have long to wait.

'Ready . . . aim . . . fire!' On the final word each standing soldier in the second row fired his musket. At the very same moment, down below on ground level, each tiny fencer (one to every human), jabbed his newly-supplied pair of compasses upwards with all his might into the rounded expanse of trouser.

Charlie and John watched in astonishment as the whole front line of the famed British square, normally secure even against cavalry attacks, leapt up almost in unison. Some held a hand against their hindquarters, others were rolling forward in the grass, and all were yelling some very rude words very loudly. It provoked gales of laughter from their colleagues. Angry words, accusations and denials were exchanged, and the major and his officers finally restored order. Everyone took up their positions again.

Including the Lilliputians.

Thorclan had got his tactics absolutely right. 'Trust me,' he'd said the previous night, 'the most vulnerable part of an army is its rear. Strike in the rear – fast and hard. It's a sitting target.'

The second, identical assault proved the truth of his words. The soldiers straightway started pushing and shoving, guns became clubs, noses became bloodied – and the fencers made good their escape. Two drummer-boys crept away to one side, still watching the escalating and thoroughly realistic fight between some over-dressed teachers, mechanics, builders and computer programmers.

The smoke was getting thicker all the time, but Jamie, Granny and Vicky sensed the growing chaos and exchanged knowing glances. Their attention was suddenly gripped by the sight and sounds of the cavalry. Bedlam had broken out. The riders were no longer in control of their mounts. Some had been thrown to the ground, and others were hanging on grimly as the steeds violently twisted and turned. The air was full of wild snortings and neighings, horses galloping frantically this way and that, scattering lines of soldiers. What had caused such a panic?

Jamie spotted the answer first, but checked his eyesight with Granny. 'Can you see anything over there by the trees?' he asked.

'Yes,' came the quiet reply, 'but I can't believe it.'

But there was no denying it. The shadowy outlines of two golden lions, magnificently larger than life, could be seen making their stately way across the battlefield. Their bodies were fully transparent except for their bold outer lines, and, as if on an African plain, the pair strode proudly across the full width of Hawkwell Field, not looking to the right or left. Jamie was no expert on lions, but he knew about these two. 'They're the ones by the South Front steps,' he said to Granny.

Vicky had seen them as well. 'What are *they* doing here?' she asked.

'No idea,' said Jamie. 'Do you think they're anything to do with Thorclan?' Granny shrugged her shoulders.

TQS Mark II were particularly proud of their contribution to the developing chaos. Reinforcements had been summoned from the tented encampment to help gather the horses, and a tight column of men, three abreast, was now pounding across the Palladian Bridge. Mr

Biddle, standing aside as they swept past, was the only one who saw the length of wire suddenly lifted up to ankle-height. Wesel and Hyroc were thrilled at the resulting pile-up, as each succeeding threesome crashed into the prone figures in front.

'That's my speciality,' said Wesel to the others as they scampered off. 'Making things fall over.'

'Mine too,' announced Melanak. Yenech looked quizzically at her. She smiled back. 'Men throwing themselves at me,' she happily explained. 'You're not the first.'

'Maybe not,' thought Yenech, 'but I *will* be the last.'

Biddle picked his way through the mass of writhing and groaning bodies, inevitably stamping on a few. He sensed this trap was Lilliputian work, but why hadn't he *seen* them? They must be nearby. A nagging fear began to play on his mind; was it possible that he *still* lacked the sight? Was Snallard an exception? 'Get out of my way, fools!' he shouted at the soldiers, kicking out. 'They're here somewhere!'

Ralph had given control of the bonfire to Nolldash and Shonntoj, who were throwing on more damp grass and old wood to deepen the smokescreen on the battlefield. Ralph himself was skirting the whole area, setting off gas-operated bird scarers that were hidden in the undergrowth. These machines emitted regular and loud explosions, good for frightening birds and for confusing military operations. Hearing gunfire from all directions, the French and the British felt surrounded; this wasn't in their briefing, and they didn't know which way to turn. Soldiers ran everywhere, shouting and yelling, falling over each other in the poor visibility and panic.

And then the squirrels arrived.

Led by the redoubtable Troyal on Walnut, and Anidox on Smoky, a swarm of at least one hundred swept *en masse* into the French artillery emplacement and caused mayhem. Picking up anything that was loose, particularly fuses, flints and paper cartridges (and some hats just for fun), they scurried hither and thither, leaping from cannon to cannon and being a complete menace. 'Give us a hand!' shouted a gunner at the Imperial Guard, who were standing to one side totally uninterested, before diving headlong after a water bottle being dragged across the grass by a furry rodent.

'No way, mate,' said one. 'More than my job's worth.'

'We're under orders,' said another. '*No* squirrels.'

'*Sacre bleu*!' shouted the horizontal soldier, at last remembering he was French. 'Who told you that?'

'Napoleon,' said a third. 'This morning.'

'See that?' said a fourth, watching a squirrel neatly pouring the contents of the water bottle down the touch-hole of a cannon. 'That *is* unusual.'

'Orders is orders,' said his neighbour. '*No squirrels.*'

Chaos reigned on Hawkwell Field. In spite of the Lilliputians' best efforts, however, the smoke was now clearing, and from his vantage point in the rat-pulled jeep, General Thorclan surveyed the scene with mounting satisfaction. On top of the Bridge, a group of Palladian professional whistlers were unhelpfully but accurately imitating the army whistle signals, orchestrating a complex military dance that would have graced any ballroom. A flutter of magpies was giving a red-coated and red-faced general a hard time. Captain Trimter was temporarily blinding people with his mirror squad, horses were still knocking people over, and a number of women camp followers were dashing around attending to the wounded. Finally, Thorclan was delighted to witness his final stratagem, as somebody 'accidentally' drove a flock of sheep through a side gate. This solid mass of woolly battering ram, moving tightly in unison, was unstoppable. Those soldiers forced back to the riverbank – and just beyond it – found the cool dip not totally unwelcome; it had been a warm afternoon.

In contrast to the hugely impressed spectators (especially three by an electric buggy), a man on the bridge was furiously angry. Grabbing a flag from a limping soldier, he waved it frantically, and it was immediately spotted by his elite squad.

'Reckon that's the signal?' said one.

'Probably,' said another.

'In that case,' said a third, 'we'd better start looking.'

'What for?'

'No idea. Anyfink wot's six inches high but *not* wiv a bushy tail.' Two Imperial Guards wandered off round the corner towards the British Worthies.

They never knew what hit them, although technically they hit each other. Down the path strode a figure dressed in Roman armour, three metres high, imperious and mean – and totally invisible to almost all. He was perfectly identical to the statue on top of the tall Cobham monument, but without the lightning conductor sticking out of his head. Picking the two men up, one in each massive hand, he swung them together head-first before dropping the limp pair on the ground. Those watching nearby were astonished that two of the soldiers had jumped at each other so fiercely. A little boy tugged a parent's hand: 'Daddy, are they *hurt*?' 'Shouldn't think so, son, it's just a show. They practise so they don't get injured. The groans are just pretend as well . . .'

The rest of the Imperial Guard were making their way up the hill towards the Gothic Temple, watched by the impressed crowds, assuming it was the grand finale of the re-enactment. The man on the bridge was urging them on. 'Find them!' he was screaming across the landscape. 'Find them all! By the *temple*! Bring them to me!'

Jamie turned to the other two. 'He *knows*,' he said sadly, almost with an air of defeat. 'He knows where they're most visible.'

'There are hundreds up there,' said Granny. 'It was the best place to watch the battle from – especially for the children.'

'There's nothing we can do,' said Vicky. 'Maybe Thorclan's got a plan.'

Thorclan hadn't, for he hadn't anticipated a cowardly assault of this kind; an elite squad moving off the battlefield in search of non-combatants. He sat back down in his jeep, despondent and feeling guilty. He knew that the Grecian army lacked the experienced troops to take on such a high-calibre unit.

His first view of the strange figures has remained in Jamie's mind even to this day. He can remember the soldiers almost reaching of the top of the slope. Then suddenly, in a moment of quiet drama, a line of seven translucent human shapes, slightly taller than life-size and golden-bronzed, majestically rose up over the brow of the hill. All in flowing robes or body-armour, some wore strange helmets or carried weapons such as swords, bows and shields. One of their number, oddly, was half the height of the others, but all their toned bodies glowed with health and vitality, their stony and impassive faces fixed for battle. Jamie thought he felt the ground shaking slightly.

'My word,' said Granny, scarcely believing her eyes. 'It's the Saxon Deities.'

'The Magnificent Seven,' said Jamie.

'Magnificent Six and a Half,' corrected Vicky. 'This should be fun.'

It was a dramatic conclusion to the Napoleonic Weekend. The French Imperial Guard showed they fully deserved their fine reputation by treating their audience to an extraordinarily imaginative display of dynamic gymnastics and self-inflicted injuries. With scant regard for health and safety, and with astonishing finesse, they pretended to double up in sudden pain, performed the most outrageous somersaults and instant standing jumps of enormous length, threw themselves backwards as if suddenly struck on the jaw, and launched themselves head-first into nearby bushes. The closing acrobatic sequence had the crowds leaping to their feet in spontaneous applause, as the heaviest soldier gave the impression of being picked up, twirled round horizontally at frightening speed like a set of helicopter rotor blades, and, after a short flight, having his landing softened by two of his men lying five metres away – presumably there for that very purpose.

The ovation continued for ten minutes, even after the whole troupe had shown impressive energy by sprinting down the hill, charging across the bridge and leaping over the nearest stretch of ha-ha.

Midway across the fields they were still running hard. And still yelling.

Mr and Mrs Thompson collected Charlie and John from amongst those straggling back from the conflict. The boys were rather subdued, and only perked up near a tent inside which a man was shouting and screaming. 'That's my father,' said John. 'He doesn't sound pleased. I'd better go back to the Manor.'

'I don't know why he's so upset,' said Mrs Thompson. 'It was a brilliant show; the first half was a bit quiet, but it was end-to-end stuff after that. Tell him he gave a lot of people a *very* entertaining afternoon.'

'I'll try,' said John. 'Bye, Charlie, see you.'

Charlie grunted the usual response, and the three Thompsons set off. 'Is it tea-time soon?' he asked.

'Not long,' said his Mum. 'What do you fancy – stirrabout? Or more pong?'

'Pizza and chips,' said Charlie. 'Though I wouldn't mind another bumper of belch.'

16 : Hopes and Fears

Although the battle had eventually ended in victory for the Lilliputians, there had been moments of real fear, most notably in the Gothic Temple.

As the Imperial Guard had drawn near, Nigriff had barely controlled the growing panic in its look-out tower. Many of the women and children, who only minutes before had been happily watching the successes of their friends and families on the battlefield, had wanted to flee their vantage point. The Archivist had struggled to persuade them that their safest option was to remain at the top of the tower; the idea didn't seem at all sensible.

'We'll be caught like rats in a trap!' had been one cry. 'Right inside a temple – where you said we'd be more *visible*! What's going on, Nigriff?' All he had been able to do was to plead with them and make promises. 'You will *not* be captured. To stay is our best hope. Stay – and *watch*.' For he alone had seen that line of glorious figures striding across the landscape from the north, beings that bore a strong resemblance to the Saxon Deities, but were larger, more powerful and full of life. Even the short one with wild hair like a sunburst.

Nobody else had seen the Magnificent Six and a Half, but of course they had all witnessed the astonishing and painful antics of the pride of the French Army. The relief of the little people at their timely rescue led to lots of handshakes and hugs, especially with Nigriff, who, to his surprise, enjoyed this outburst of emotions.

'Okay, Nigriff,' said Selbol, a dark-haired Palladian woman. 'What *did* happen to those men down there? You obviously know something.'

'I appreciate your trust in me,' Nigriff said. 'It is rare for the words of an Archivist to be given such respect and authority in a crisis.' He bit his lip and thought hard; maybe now was the time to tell these good people. It couldn't do any harm, and they had shown their faith in him by remaining in the Temple. He decided to be completely frank with them.

'There are two important words you must remember,' he said. '*Restoration* and *destruction*.' This instruction only produced puzzled looks. 'It's a phrase from an old document in the archives. I have come to believe it indicates that as Malplaquet and its buildings are restored, there will be increasing danger for its inhabitants. For all of us.'

'Any *more* good news?' was a sarcastic comment from the back. 'Sorry, this history lesson is all very interesting, but I need to go now.'

'Of course,' said Nigriff. 'I understand. I'm sorry to have kept you.' And having received that gracious apology, Snallard slipped away down the gloom of the spiral staircase.

Discussion began about the strange lights seen amongst the acrobatic soldiers. A few Lilliputians had noticed darting flashes and unusual brilliances swirling around, and others had noticed a vague alteration in the atmosphere, a shimmering of the daylight. They wanted an answer from Nigriff. He chose his words carefully, partly because he couldn't yet fully explain to himself what he had just seen.

'The details are not totally clear,' Nigriff began. 'But I would refer you to suggestions I have previously made about *energies* at Malplaquet. Putting it simply, in words of under five syllables – there are forces here beyond our rational comprehension.'

'Whose side are these "forces" on?' asked Seswym, holding her two young sons close.

'I can arrive at only one conclusion from recent events,' replied Nigriff. They're on *our* side.'

One boy clapped, and the other shouted a loud, 'Yes!'

The mother was more cautious. 'If that's so, why are we having all these problems? It's my kids I worry about.'

'There are promises of our *eventual* safety,' said Nigriff, looking round at the assembled Lilliputians, 'of our ultimate happiness. But I fear there will be yet more struggles.'

'Like today,' said Selbol. Nigriff murmured his agreement.

'Although it *was* fun,' said Byonnops chirpily. 'I could cope with that again. Are you still convinced, Nigriff, that this Biddle person is the main problem?'

'He *is* our primary adversary,' said Nigriff. 'Especially now that, as the new Property Manager, he has been given some authority over our world.' The people looked sombre; accepting this judgement about Biddle was easy. His final shouts of 'Bring them to me!' had echoed sharply across Hawkwell Field, initiating their fright in the look-out tower.

'However,' continued Nigriff, a smile appearing on his lips, 'what has been very clear today is that he is significantly *limited.* He *cannot,* repeat *cannot,* see us. Whether that will change or not is impossible to say, but I know this much. We should *not* be fearful of him; one day we *will* defeat him.'

'When?' asked Selbol.

'That I do not know,' answered Nigriff. 'But being a librarian by inclination and training, I have a profound sense that he is living on *borrowed* time. The day *is* coming.'

'So are you looking forward to next term?' asked Vicky, watching Jamie pulling firmly on the oars of last summer's birthday present. It was one of his first excursions this year, and he was enjoying showing off his expertise on the Eleven-Acre Lake.

'Pretty much,' said Jamie. 'All apart from the tennis.'

'Tennis? What's wrong with that? It's usually good fun.'

'Not the way Gratton plays it, with his Terminator. He's frightening. I had to go to his indoor sessions last term, and his serves dislodged a couple of breeze blocks in the wall and eventually ripped the net apart. Have you ever seen him with Hobbes up on the sports field? The man's a maniac.'

'I'm sure you'll think of something,' said Vicky. 'Like last time.'

Jamie did think about it and decided to change the subject. 'I still can't work out what happened with those seven – or six and a half – statues. Ralph is *absolutely* sure they didn't move?'

'Totally,' she replied, lazily dragging a finger through the water and watching the ripples feathering out behind her. 'This isn't slowing you down, is it?'

'Very funny,' said Jamie. 'Just don't get any blood on my boat when a vazedir grabs his lunch.'

Vicky swiftly retrieved the vulnerable finger with a start. 'Seriously, Ralph doesn't really get it. He could see *both* groups at the same time – the stone ones still standing in their usual place over by the trees, and the bigger ones chucking those blokes around by the Gothic Temple.'

'It's so weird,' said Jamie. 'It was bad enough when some statues were just saying things . . .'

'That "oops" was not at all funny,' said Vicky.

'. . . but now they've started wrestling with humans, you wonder what they're going to do next.'

'I *did* like those lions though,' said Vicky. 'I made a point of going along the South Front today. I thought they might be at least purring, but I couldn't hear a thing. Probably just as well.'

'And best of all,' puffed Jamie, hoping that Vicky wasn't noticing how hard the rowing was becoming, 'is that I reckon Biddle didn't see anything. Saxon statues, lions, Lilliputians – nothing. He hasn't got a hope. I don't know why he doesn't give up.'

'So are you saying we've just about won?' asked Vicky hopefully.

'Not sure,' said Jamie. 'But we're so much stronger than him. It's like we've won some battles – but maybe not the war. Not until he disappears for good.' He paused. 'Can we stop for a bit?'

'Why?'

'The, er . . . view. It's really nice here.'

'Sure. You could get your breath back as well.' She smiled. 'The other good thing is that I haven't caught a whiff of Smelly Newbold recently. Biddle must be stuck for help nowadays.' A ripple splashed against the side of the boat. 'Oh, that reminds me,' she said. 'I met Thorclan this morning. He says he's being decorated in the next Assembly.'

'What is it this time?'

'Apparently it's a very old honour, really impressive.'

'And it's called?'

'Prime Liberator of Peoples.'

Jamie worked out the acronym and burst out laughing. General Thorclan – GLOB, SCAB, PLOP. What a man. What a hero. But to be fair, he had just defeated both the British and the French in a Napoleonic conflict, and what other military leader could claim the same? It was the least he deserved.

Sunsets at Malplaquet can be spectacular. Across its acres of open landscape, the sun gently slips down behind darkening silhouettes of trees and temples, swathes of colour reflecting off quiet lakes. Seated on the bench before the Temple of Friendship, Granny and Nigriff were enjoying the slow and measured descent of evening.

'I gather Thorclan is delighted with his latest award,' said Granny smiling. 'He's really come on this last year. Like lots of other people.'

Nigriff nodded. 'Many of these changes are immensely reassuring, Madam.'

'Which ones are you thinking of, Nigriff?'

'Only today I overheard two young children arguing. One, regrettably, was an Elysian, making hurtful remarks about the Palladian ancestry of the other. To my relief, the Elysian mother appeared and scolded her son. 'We're all *Lilliputians* now,' she said. That made my heart sing.'

'The spirit of the new Empire,' said Granny. 'It's going to be wonderful.'

'Indeed, Madam, one hopes that it will be as wonderful as our vision of Lilliput. However, in the meantime,' added Nigriff, 'battle-lines are hardening. Visitors are increasing. More restoration. More . . .' and here he paused to gather his thoughts. He looked up wistfully towards the sun, now barely visible above the distant trees. 'Perhaps I should for the moment not continue. Despite all the difficulties and upheavals, we *have* made considerable progress towards our final goal. Furthermore, as I sit here with you, I know that amongst all the chances and uncertainties of our life here, *one* thing will *never* change.'

'What's that, Nigriff?' asked Granny.

He leaned back against the wall of the temple, its worn upper stones glowing a soft rose in the gentle light. 'It's how this all began, dearest Madam,' he said. 'With the Warmth of Friendship. And may it always be so.'

'Do you know what's funny?' said Dad over supper. His sons looked up doubtfully; it almost inevitably wouldn't be funny, but someone had to respond. Mum did the honours. 'What is?'

'That battle,' he said. 'It was below the Gothic Temple. Funny, really.'

Charlie gave a low sigh; another amazingly *unfunny* moment from Dad. He was shocked to then hear Jamie ask, 'Why?' Did his brother have no table manners? Did he not realise that it would only encourage his father?

'*Think*, Jamie. What did I tell you recently about why Malplaquet was built?'

'To be like a painting,' said Jamie, realising too late (and that it was his fault) that the family meal had become a lesson.

'Good. That's the *Art* reason. What do you know about the Politics one?'

'Nothing.'

Now it was Dad who was shocked. 'And we're spending all that money . . . ?'

'No,' said Mum. '*We're* not. *Granny* is – and we should be grateful.'

'Anyway,' continued Dad, 'Malplaquet wasn't just meant to be a painting, it was also built to make clear the political opinions of its owners. The gardens are like a stone version of a party political broadcast.'

Charlie grimaced. Those things were bad enough on television, and now he was being told that they often walked right through one? How appalling was that?

Jamie, however, was becoming interested. 'So how did they explain their ideas?'

'They set up statues of people they respected, and lots of inscriptions mentioned their party's beliefs.'

'What *sort* of beliefs?' asked Jamie again. Charlie groaned.

'Freedom mainly,' said Dad.

Jamie stopped his fork halfway to his mouth. 'Seriously?'

'That's why it was funny about the Gothic Temple,' continued his father. 'It represents that belief better than anything else at Malplaquet. It was built in an old, gothic, style to remind people of how their ancestors lived in freedom; it was even dedicated to "The Liberty of Our Ancestors". It's odd that the battle took place nearby. You know, people becoming free after a big fight.'

'Sorry,' said Jamie, swallowing hard. 'Got to go.' He dashed out and ran upstairs.

'Me too,' garbled Charlie. Once inside his brother's bedroom, he shut the door behind him and leant against it.

'Right,' he said firmly. '*Now* you're going to tell me.'

'Tell you what?' asked Jamie, surprised at the intrusion and demand.

'About the little people,' said Charlie, watching for his brother's reaction.

Jamie's heart missed a beat, but he tried to play it cool and paused before answering. 'Which little people?'

'The ones that stabbed our men in the backside during the battle. The ones that explain why you're always hanging round Granny and her dolls. The ones that explain why you're now blushing and looking guilty.'

There was no escaping it.

The game was up.

Jamie was going to have to tell him.

The gardens of Chackmore Manor were taking a beating from a late-April squall. Bursts of heavy rain were peppering the tormented lake, the scrawny daffodils and tulips were ducking and diving like boxers, and tall hedges were leaning to and fro as if in a heavy sea. The owner stared out the window, his mood as angry as the elements.

The disaster at Hawkwell Field still embittered him. Not only had he failed to catch any Lilliputians, he had also discovered that they were far more resourceful than he'd suspected – and far more lucky. There was no way he could have anticipated the sheep and squirrels turning up. He resolved not to be caught out like that again, and made a mental note to propose 'Squirrel Extermination' at the next Garden Management meeting.

Worst of all, however, was the infuriating fact that he'd failed to see any more of the tiny people. He must *still* be cursed with this particular blindness. Why?

He strode over to the double doors of his favoured cupboard, pulled them open and gazed into the hard eyes of his ancestor. Under a deep compulsion, he grabbed hold of its shoulders and gently dragged it closer to the front, willing Captain Biddle to assist his poor descendant in some way. There had to be an answer. He leaned forward, pressing cold unforgiving forehead to forehead.

The rain continued to hurl itself against the windows, the climbing plants beating out a repetitive rhythm on the glass. Jedekiah gradually became aware of this steady tapping like a sharp percussion, and then realised that no wild gale would cause such a uniform beat.

Moving to the window, he looked for the guilty branches and found nothing. Indeed, the noise was now fainter. As he returned to the centre of the room, away from the outside fury, it grew louder again. Still the knocking, most regular, at intervals. Bemused, he opened the door slightly. Still nothing.

Until he looked down.

Snallard was at the base of the door, putting a shoe back on.

'Hello,' he said. 'Can I come in?'

Biddle was still so angry at the world in general, that he was sorely tempted to say something rude to this irritation, but he remembered in time that he needed to be nice to it. He beckoned him in, placed him on his desk, and settled himself in his chair. The two collaborators were at eye-level.

'How did you get here?' was Biddle's first question.

'I got a lift,' said Snallard. 'With your son.'

'What?' barked Biddle, unable to contain his shock. 'Did he see you?'

Snallard shook his head. 'I hid in his backpack after school, and hopped out when he left it in his bedroom. No-one knows I'm here. Have you got any marzipan?'

'No,' said Biddle curtly, cross at the impertinence of the creature. Then, remembering its usefulness, added, 'Or I *might* have. Why have you come?'

'I have uncovered some facts,' he announced proudly.

Biddle was torn between curiosity about the information and

frustration at being indebted to such a pathetic being. He forced himself to say, 'I am delighted to hear that. What do you wish to tell me?'

'This information comes straight from the "great man" himself,' said Snallard. 'From Nigriff. It is *totally* reliable. Told to me personally, in a situation of great personal risk, I might add. The only problem is that my memory can be hazy, but marzipan helps. Especially Wiltshire's.'

The Lord of Chackmore Manor was finding it hard not to treat this arrogant specimen as it deserved. Why should he allow this minion to treat the descendant of the noble Captain John Biddle in such a demeaning manner? He felt like bringing his fist down hard on the desk, but the thought of some possibly important news restrained him. He coolly opened a drawer, chose a small dyed apple from a tray, and handed it over.

Snallard's little eyes lit up. 'As beautiful as I remember,' he said with glee. He took a large bite and began to chew.

Biddle watched him eat, conscious of a rising fury within. This playing around had better be worth it. If it wasn't . . . well, he would be needing another informer.

After the longest three minutes of Biddle's life, the meal was over, and Snallard began to lick his hands. 'Delicious,' he acknowledged, and sat down. 'It is about Malplaquet,' he said. 'It appears that some changes are causing problems for Nigriff and his little gang.'

'No doubt the increased visitor numbers,' responded Biddle, regretting ever giving any time and space to this irrelevant pipsqueak.

'No,' said Snallard, enjoying being able to correct his patron, and unaware of how much he was playing with fire. 'Three words. Restoration and destruction.'

'Really?' said Biddle, eyeing the lunatic sat on his desk. 'Tell me more.'

'Nigriff is pretending otherwise, but he's *really* worried. He told me this; as the temples are gradually *restored*, the people face greater and greater *danger*.'

Biddle couldn't believe his luck – or his own folly in not realising it sooner. He now saw the whole thing in a flash. Of course – restoring the temples. It was so obvious. First of all, the smarter buildings attract more visitors and disturb the Lilliputians. That would annoy them. But secondly, the very process itself of restoration would inevitably uncover their homes and hiding-places. The midgets would be running in all directions, and there would be fewer places to hide – and at the same time more people to avoid.

This was great news.

Furthermore, Biddle realised with excitement, if he himself could still see this one in front of him, surely one or two others might be visible as well? Maybe his sight wasn't as bad as he had just been fearing. He swiftly cut short the discussion, claiming the need to talk to his staff, but happily gave Snallard another lump before dumping him on the window-sill.

'You mustn't come here again,' he explained. 'It's much too far.' Sliding the sash window up, the two of them instantly recoiled from the onslaught of the furious wind and rain. Snallard braced himself and stamped forwards head down, holding tightly on to his sweet reward. He disappeared into the foliage.

Behind them, papers were flying off Biddle's desk, noticeboards were flapping madly, and a tall, top-heavy standard lamp took the full force of the wind that was channelling in through the gap. As if in slow motion, Biddle watched it tip one way then the other, before finally making its inevitable descent towards the open doors of his prized cupboard. The one that contained a priceless possession.

'*No-o!*' he shouted, but he was too far away. He could do nothing. The large shade caught the bust a glancing blow, causing it to over-balance and fall forwards off the edge. It hit the floor with a heavy, dead thud and a sharp crack.

Ignoring the whirlwind sweeping round the room, Biddle sank to his knees by the broken head, hardly daring to look. It had been in his family for generations; it was his life, his purpose. Plucking up the courage to check for damage more closely, he saw a transverse line, a faint mark running across the top of the head, from ear to ear. He'd never noticed it before; presumably this slight fracture had been smoothed over in the final stages of craftsmanship. Biddle slowly lifted a cracked piece of stone from alongside this fault line.

What he saw underneath made him gasp and sit back.

It was a mass of thin grey fibres.

Instinctively he knew it was hair.

Human hair.

Captain John Biddle's hair.

It was a full ten minutes before Jedekiah Biddle could get to his feet. Trembling, and still in a daze, he arose and shut the window, not noticing the soaked furnishings nearby. Returning to the broken image on the floor, he steeled himself to reveal more of what had been entombed for centuries inside the grim mask. Bit by bit, he began to gingerly and reverently prise away each loose segment, like a surgeon peeling bandages from his handiwork.

The object he revealed was beyond description. Not a real head, but something far worse; it was a clumsy and ugly attempt to rebuild one. More clumps of hair, grey and matted. Some crown and facial bones. Wax and plaster re-modelling. Two old misty glass eyes, cracked and yellowing. Porcelain teeth amongst original stained ones. Painted colouration, dirty brown and dull red.

It was a macabre and frightening jigsaw, but it was also the mortal remains of Captain John Biddle, rescuer of Gulliver and kidnapper of Lilliputians.

The embodiment of their destruction had returned.

On his knees before his ancestor and inspiration, Jedekiah Biddle was solemnly pushing away the shards, fully revealing the ugly and gruesome relic, and also aware of a surge of power welling up from deep within himself. He was no longer alone. Destiny had united the servant with the Master, and he now knew that their mission would prevail.

Nothing could possibly stop the two of them.